an MPOWELL

R.O.C HARD

a novel by
$$Mike

The life of a
True Hustler...

outskirtspress
DENVER, COLORADO

Outskirts Press, Inc.
http://www.outskirtspress.com

ISBN: 978-1-4787-3023-1

Outskirts Press and the "OP" logo are trademarks belonging to Outskirts Press, Inc.

PRINTED IN THE UNITED STATES OF AMERICA

Dedication

This book is loosely based on true events and street personalities from my past experiences. In no way am I meaning to glorify the streets. I am simply certified to tell a familiar story. I have come a long way in my personal life and hope every hustler will follow my lead. Please read this book and like it- but understand that there is a better way...

David "Dek" King
Derrick "Supreme" Danner
Until we meet again…

Free my cousins…
Marvin "Veen" Powell
Kevin "P- Double" Parks

IN THE BEGINNING

O leanne's family moved from Georgia to Rochester, New York in search for a better life. One that was promised to be filled with more opportunities than the old fashioned south had to offer. They soon settled on the northeast side of the city in a rugged neighborhood called, Marketview Heights. Decades passed by and soon the Miller family were no longer strangers to the city.

It's no secret that Rochester, most often represented as the R.O.C, bred whores and pimps, drug dealers and killers. It is a city that held the number one murder rate per population since '88. Marketview Heights is located on the east side of Rochester. It's a small rectangular shaped area of about fifteen blocks and alleys, dissected in the middle by one long two lane street called, the "Strip". And without a question this is the worst neighborhood that Rochester has to offer. Here, everything is for sale from sex to crack, and guns to heroin. Crack addicts roam the Strip twenty-four seven in search of their next fix. The Strip didn't get its name for being a place where prostitutes are stationed to solicit would be costumers, but actually it comes from the fact that this is where it all happens. Anything you need could be found on the Strip, legal or illegal, dead smack in the middle of Marketview Heights.

Neighborhoods like this are sometimes the only place for low-class black and hispanic families to raise their children. Anybody would choose somewhere better than Marketview Heights to call their home. Only if better was an option. It's almost like these inner city ghettos are the modern day slave plantations for minorities. The majority of the time it's the children who really suffer. They never get a fair chance to prosper. Never have a chance to be guided in the seldom traveled path of success. And as soon as they turn to the Rochester streets for acceptance, the brothers on the block are eagerly waiting to put crack in the young boy's hands, and to defile the young girls mind and bodies.

This was the environment that Oleanne inherited once moving to Rochester. Being subject to these harsh circumstances; very few people, especially women, are able to maintain their sanity and not fall victim. This is indeed a very difficult thing to do. Oleanne hasn't yet become swallowed up by the terrible crack epidemic of the late 80's, but since a teenager she has suffered from dipsomania. Her love for alcohol escalated around the time she conceived her first child who she named, Tymer Miller. He was born seven years ago. She quickly let the struggle of being a young single mother get the best of her. She turned to liquor, wine, and beer as an instant source of comfort when times got too rough. To her the alcohol was all she needed to wash the pain away. Soon she let herself fall to the point of border line poverty. Along with the recent birth of her second child Kimberly, rats and roaches were as much a part of the household as her children.

It's a shame that her son Tymer Miller will never know his father. In fact, if his dad was to walk up and slap the hell out of him he'd never of known who hit him. Oleanne Miller, known as Anne, doesn't even have a clue to who is the father of her one year old daughter Kimberly. It could be out of about (being nice) six different men. Not even including the magnitude of partners she forgot about during her drunken one night stands.

Any man who would claim children by Anne was subject to being the laughing stock of the city. This was not because she is an ugly woman. Anne still has the reflection of a beautiful model if you could see past the effects of all the alcohol she has consumed. But the true reason no man could confess to having a baby with her is because of the fact that her moral standards are as low as zero degrees on a cold winter day.

Anne is brown-skinned with a pair of the most beautiful hazel eyes God has ever blessed any human with. She has a sexy curvaceous body with long silky hair that manages to hang down the middle of her back. The sexy outfits she wears always do a great job at revealing the curves of her lovely body. She never hesitated to flaunt the thickness of her southern shape around in the hood. Anne just loves sex with a passion and everyone in Marketview Heights knows how easy she is to sleep with.

Anne was only twelve years old when her mother Rose passed away from heart failure. Rose was the only family living in Rochester Anne had left besides her older brother, Freddie, who was forced to take care of her. Soon Anne began having sex with boys and drinking alcohol. She was the prime example of an out of control teenager. Living between the streets and Freddie's house Anne continued this lifestyle throughout her twenties.

All any man in the hood needed to have sex with Anne was about twenty dollars and a bottle of gin. Once you provided these things there really was no limit. However, Anne was never caught drunk enough to give up free sex. It may have been cheap, but it was never totally free. Her brother Freddie was a retired pimp. All of her life he schooled her about having sex for free. During his stint as a well-known pimp he'd seen the sweetest ladies get turned out and suddenly become the nastiest women alive, for the small price of next to nothing. "Anne, if you're going to be out here fucking with these sorry ass hustlers you better learn how to get paid for it. Nobody will take care of your children if you don't," he'd tell her. It wasn't the best advice to give his baby sister, but knowing the game, meant knowing what she was up against.

At the young age of twenty-six Anne has all of the odds stacked up against her. A female who was once a bright little girl is now a promiscuous alcoholic with two bad children. Her situation plus the environment she lives in is one that spells out to pure destruction.

The little boy of hers Tymer and his sister Kimberly are innocent victims of the choices their mother made. They will now face the challenges of not falling into the same struggles as she did. Drugs will be at their fingertips to either sell or use. Guns will be around to either be fired or used to harm one of them. Older men will try and lure Tymer into the "false" life of selling crack. They will prey on Kimberly as soon as she reaches puberty and her little body begins to develop. School would be an option for both, but only if Anne enforces it as a priority.

In the city of Rochester, New York drugs, guns, broken homes, and poor education is provided to the ghettos. Some strive to overcome and make it out, but realistically many never even stood a chance. Very few people actually make it out of the ghetto. How many brothers ever leave the hood without a bullet wound or doing a stiff prison sentence first? How many females leave without getting pregnant at a young age or succumbing to life on the system?

Here in Marketview Heights children grow with the do or die mentality and vow to escape the slums by any means. Anne's two kids are no different. They are subject to the same struggles. And in this day and time the world is only getting worse. It's getting harder and harder to survive in the R.O.C...

CHAPTER ONE
THE SALE

Fifteen Years Later...

"It's one thing to grow up in a tough neighborhood, but to rise and to succeed is entirely a different story. People so often fall victim to the harsh drugs, while some make terrible decisions and end up losing their lives prematurely. Others watch and learn preparing themselves for which ever road life leads them too. Those are the ones who become prosperous even when doing wrong. The only problem is that the better you do, and the more you seem to achieve there is always someone waiting, plotting, and ready to bring you down..."

It was a normal freezing cold Tuesday on one of Rochester's winter nights. Due to the weather and the late time the Marketview Heights area was somewhat deserted. The only people who would have an interest in roaming these cold streets were drug addicts, hustlers, and prostitutes. And for many of them tonight was just too cold.

A tall white undercover police officer nervously stood alone in a dark alley. He was a ten year veteran of the Rochester Drug Enforcement Unit. Although he'd been used to this kind of drug enforcement, he was still trembling in his boots. Not because of the freezing cold snow that was falling; he was scared because he was undercover in the notorious Marketview Heights neighborhood. This was an assignment that very few officers looked forward too. In many cases this act alone of standing in an alley at night could have been deadly.

The undercover constantly watched his back as he waited for a local crack head to return with two twenty dollar bags of crack. He'd cleverly persuaded the unsuspecting crack addict to go and purchase the drugs from a well-known drug house on the opposite street. During the winter months many of the drug dealers would rent apartments to sell their cocaine from. It was the Drug Enforcement Unit's duty to locate these spots, conduct a forty-five day investigation, and finally find a way to make a purchase from the suspected drug house. If in fact a purchase could be made, it would be enough to activate the search warrant issued by a judge.

The undercover appeared to be alone, but just around the corner was his backup. The jump out squad was huddled closely together in the back of a white caravan. Just behind them were five regular police cruisers parked in a straight line with their lights off. Each officer was waiting for one thing and that was for the undercover to confirm that a sell was made at the targeted location.

———————◦«◦»◦———————

"Kiki, you don't be letting me hit it right. I mean every time I try to get up in there good you always running. I remember one time half of your body was hanging off of the damn bed. Then you got the nerve to tell me you don't be cumming. How do you expect for me to make you cum if you don't let me do my thing?" the male voice said into his Sprint cell phone.

"Please Kilo, you be trying to kill me. What do you expect? Sometimes you be fucking me like you haven't had any pussy in years... Don't worry because if you come home right now I'll let you do what you want to me. You can have your way. If I start running from your dick just hold me down and make me cry!" Kiki instructed in her most sexiest voice.

"I think you playing with me."

"No I'm not. That's my word you could fuck me how you want and I won't complain!" Kiki said.

"So when I get home you going to finally let me kill it?" Kilo asked in disbelief.

"Yep you'll see."

"Why did you decide to change your mind? For years you've been saying make love to me. Don't treat me like a slut and now it's make you cry?"

"I just want to please my man. I'm tired of hearing my friend Renee brag about how her man takes advantage of her, but I hardly let you do anything you want during sex. I want to make sure you are getting everything from home that you could get in those streets," Kiki explained.

"Girl you already give me all that I need at home. It is perfect, but don't get me wrong I am coming there to give you a hell of a story to tell your friends!" Kilo said, followed by laughter. "Kiki hold on for one second…"

Kilo placed his cell phone on the table in front of him. He leaned forward and picked up a snub-nosed .38 revolver that was resting on top of a pile of twenty dollar bills. With his favorite gun in hand Kilo reached and grabbed a hand full of small plastic bags that were filled with see through crack cocaine. They were atop a napkin with about fifty more bags.

Kilo got up from the couch and headed down a short hallway that led to a small bedroom. The room was completely empty except for a queen-sized bed that occupied the far left corner. This bed was used when Kilo or one of his boys had a freak that was ready and willing to have sex. Sometimes the house would be filled with niggahs from Marketview Heights that were waiting for their turn to be called into the room. Most females that came to Kilo's spot were known as deuces; women who didn't mind having sex with more than one hustler at a time. This was a normal occurrence for the hustlers of Marketview Heights. If you were getting money females lined up at your door ready and more than willing to fuck you and your whole crew if requested.

Kilo slowly crept up to the only window in the bedroom. Most of the entire window was covered by a sheet of wood. The only part that wasn't covered was the very bottom. There were two holes drilled in the middle of the wood. This allowed a person to be able to see outside, but at the same time conceal the identity of the person inside. Kilo peeped through the small hole, and yelled in a disguised voice, "Who is that?"

"Kilo, its Snowman. Let me get two of those healthy things?" the man on the opposite side of the window said as he recognized Kilo's voice.

"Don't be saying my fucking name! Next time your fiend ass won't get shit," Kilo quickly yelled back.

Snowman was a local crack head from the area. His hustle was shoveling driveways and sidewalks for the residents in the hood. Anytime he made enough money he was sure to come and buy crack from Kilo. The bags were always humungous and Kilo had the best product in Marketview Heights.

"I'm sorry Kilo... You want me to come back in the morning to shovel this sidewalk?" Snowman asked.

"Hell no, and if you say my name again I'm coming out there to punch you in your fucking face!"

"Sorry man, sorry," Snowman pleaded as he attempted to slide Kilo two twenty dollar bills through the window.

"Whose money is this?" Kilo asked wisely before he took it.

"Mines... I mean... I got the white boy at my house. He said if he likes it he'll spend all night. I know he's going to like it because you keep that good shit," Snowman said stuttering. He was obviously lying.

"Snowman I swear to God if you don't know this fucking white boy I have bullets with your name on them. Do you see this fucking gun niggah?" Kilo asked as he flashed the shiny chrome pistol under the window. Kilo knew that Snowman sometimes would buy crack for people he didn't know when he really wanted to get high. This was exactly how a lot of hustlers caught indirect sale charges; by fucking with those thirsty ass crack heads. But giving Snowman the benefit of the doubt Kilo gave him two bags in exchange for his forty dollars.

"Hell yea I see that big ass gun. Man what is that a forty-five? A three-fifty-seven? Boy you could knock a bitch whole head off with that shit... Kilo, where is Rah Rah?" Snowman asked as he tossed the two plastic bags into his mouth.

"Hold on niggah you still saying my name? I'm about to come beat..."

Snowman didn't wait around. He grabbed his shovel that was leaning up against the yellow house and hauled ass, falling down in the snow twice as he ran away.

Kilo walked back into the smoke filled living room smiling. He replaced the gun back on the table and tossed the remaining bags of crack he had in his hand back onto the napkin. Just in case, he stuffed the two twenty dollar bills he'd gotten from Snowman into his pants pocket. Kilo then grabbed his cell phone, and then fell back onto the couch all in one motion. "Hello!" he called back into the phone.

"So when are you coming home kilo?" Kiki asked impatiently.

"I'll be there in a minute. I'm waiting for Lil' Rah Rah to come back," Kilo explained.

"Where is he? Doesn't he get paid to stay in the house?" she asked confused.

"Yea, but he has to wash his ass sometimes. Why are you questioning me anyways? You just better be ready for me when I get there."

Kilo always made sure that he protected Kiki from his street life. That included her knowing about certain things he was into. A lot of street figure's downfalls were not being able to separate their personal life from their businesses. Even the world's most success-ful hustlers and many brutal killers have made the grave mistake of letting their women know too much. All Kiki needed to know was that her house, tuition, and living expenses were all paid for.

Kilo had a baby sister named Kimberly. She was murdered at the tender age of nine. To this day Kilo could never get over the memories of watching his sister bleed to death in his young arms.

One night little Kimberly decided to sneak outside alone to play in front of the house. Her mother was upstairs in the bedroom with the door locked, and was busy getting her brains fucked out at the time. Little Kilo heard the screeching tires from the living room. Then he heard the first shots. He frantically looked around for his sister. He noticed the front door was wide open. The sound of gun fire continued. Kilo ran outside and found his sister lying on the sidewalk in a pool of her own blood. Kimberly had been shot once in her small chest.

From that night forward Kilo vowed to protect every women in his life, unfortunately, his mother Anne too.

Kilo resented his mother for being a poor excuse for a black woman. He blamed her for the death of his sister. With all of his rage and frustration Kilo turned to the streets at the age of fifteen. He began to live between the streets and his Uncle Freddie's home. Soon he earned the name Kilo from the hood. This name was given to him because he was the youngest person in Marketview Heights that was buying kilograms of cocaine at a time.

At twenty-two now Kilo is already recognized as an O.G.; origi-nal gangster that is. Before the money Kilo was terrorizing the hus-tlers in the hood. He was robbing anybody that looked like they had money and shooting anyone who refused to give it up. He just slowed down from his violent ways recently when he finally per-suaded Kiki to move in with him. Kilo recently purchased a home in the suburbs of Rochester, New York.

Kiki whose real name is Keisha has been Kilo's girlfriend for years. They share a real childhood love story. Aside from being romantically involved they had a sister-brother like bond also. Keisha witnessed Kilo grow up in the worst conditions that a person could ever face. Her family was always financially stable and it hurt that her boyfriend was so poor. She used to steal money from her parents just to buy Kilo cloths and sneakers. She had to save Kilo and his sister plates of food because she knew that Anne rarely cooked dinner. At the time Kilo couldn't understand why Kiki loved him so much. All he knew was that he loved her to death. Hands down Kiki was the best thing that ever happened to Tymer Miller.

"Excuse me! I shouldn't have asked Daddy. I know how you are about your personal business," Kiki said apologizing. "But I am so wet and horny, and I know you're going to take all night."

Before Kilo could respond there was a knock at the door.

CHAPTER TWO
THE BUST

"**D**ealing with life and success it's very hard to determine when and where obstacles will arise. This makes it very difficult to prepare. There is a thing called, The Element of Surprise, this is where the predator lies in wait for the perfect time to attack its prey; a time when it will be totally taken off guard. When this method of attack is applied correctly, the reaction time of the victim becomes a matter of life or death. In the case of hustling it is a matter of jail and freedom; in which cases, only the elite are capable of making wise decisions under the nerve racking pressures of the element of surprise..."

Snowman stopped between two abandoned houses to catch his breath after running from the spot. He watched his back to make sure Kilo wasn't coming. He knew that it was easy to piss Kilo off, and when you did, running was the best thing to do.

Snowman crouched down in a corner between a small green city garbage can and a blue house that looked like fire had destroyed it some time ago. He slipped the two bags from under his tongue and spit them into his dirty hand. His eyes became large as two baseballs as he stared at the small white rocks that filled each bag to its limit. He thought long and hard about whether or not he should return to the white man who'd sent him to buy the crack.

He looked in the direction of his house, which was only two blocks away, and then he looked in the direction of the alley where the white guy was waiting. Snowman then looked down at the all so tempting bags of crack he held in his palm and decided on returning to the white man under the notion that he could possibly want more.

Snowman pulled a book of matches from his soiled coat pocket, ripped it in half, and then stuck the part holding the match sticks back into his pocket. He folded the piece of paper horizontally. Snowman nervously opened each of the two bags of crack and poured out half of the rocks onto the folded paper. He hurried up, closed both bags, and then stuffed his "fee" deep into his coat pocket. Racing against time Snowman jumped up and ran through the backyard. As he jumped the small fence that led to the alley you could hear the loud barking of dogs that were guarding other yards.

Snowman walked slowly up the dark alley. It was illuminated in certain parts by street lights. As Snowman approached he saw the white man standing impatiently in the middle of the dangerous alley. He was using his breath to heat up his cold hands.

For the first time Snowman mused to himself about how odd it was that this weird looking white man was willing to wait alone in this dark alley at twelve o'clock in the night. Didn't he know where he was? The average white person would be terrified to even walk through Marketview Heights during broad daylight, let alone stand around in one of the many deadly alleys by themselves. Not to mention that the man was wearing an expensive brown Carhartt jacket. Snowman also knew that he definitely had never seen him around before. He knew that Kilo would kill him if he ever brought dirty money to his spot. However, Snowman thought, '*I have some free crack. This white boy is my man!*'

"Hey buddy! What took you so long? Did you get the stuff?" the undercover asked excitedly. He was playing the role of a crack head to the tee.

"You know I did. Here you go," Snowman said while handing over the two pinched bags of crack.

"Is it real? Do I have to taste it? I've been sold some bullshit around here before," the officer said.

"Man is you serious? I'm Snowman. Taste it if you want too. Everybody around here knows that I'm straight up man. If you want you could even come to my house and smoke. It's only a few streets over," Snowman offered as the undercover briefly examined the bags.

"That's okay buddy. I got to share this with a few people back at my place. It looks good though. I'd better get going," the undercover said as he gave Snowman a hard pat on his left shoulder.

Usually Snowman would have asked for a little rock or a few dollars for his services, but being that he had already stolen half of each bag, he didn't bother. He didn't want the white man looking at the bags too long then becoming curious as to why they were so small for twenty dollars a pop. So with a smile Snowman just watched as the white man disappeared into the darkness...

The knocking on the front door continued.

"Kiki I'll be home as soon as possible. Remember what you told me," Kilo said rushing her off of the phone so that he could answer the door.

"I will. You just hurry up and get here. I need you so bad. I'm wearing this sexy ass lingerie, and I got something special planned for you," Kiki said enticingly.

They both said, "I love you," and then Kilo hung up and started towards the front door. The knocking came to the door again. Kilo peered through the peephole and saw into the familiar face of his worker Lil' Rah Rah. He smiled to himself at the pleasant thoughts of finally being able to go home and sex his queen.

"What's up Kilo?" Rah Rah said as he saluted Kilo with a handshake. He was a young light-skinned kid with small freckles covering his cheeks. His red slanted eyes left very little doubt about his seriousness.

"Not shit," Kilo said as he quickly relocked the pad locks and replaced the two-by-fours over the door.

"Why was Snowman running out of the yard like that? He almost busted his ass when he slid on that slippery ass ice on the sidewalk," Rah Rah said.

"Oh. He came to the window and kept on yelling my damn name. He thought I was coming out there to kick his ass, but I didn't fuck with him though," Kilo answered. Rah Rah busted out into laughter. He admired Kilo and always laughed at his jokes.

Kilo sat back on the coach and started gathering up all of the drug money from the table. There were piles of hundreds, fifties, and twenty dollar bills. Rah Rah walked over to the window and stood there looking out through the blinds. He could see the street, and anybody who came into the yard and was going to the back window. This was the post he usually assumed during the nights when he was at the spot alone.

"Seriously, Rah' its forty-five bags right here. Call me when you get down to around ten or fifteen. The fiends have been coming all night so don't be falling asleep and shit. I know you, once you get some of that good weed in your system you out like a light. But don't let it happen tonight son. You hear me?"

"It won't. I got my little bitch coming over at one o'clock when her peoples definitely sleep for the night. So you know I'll be in the back room fucking anyways," Rah Rah said from the window with a smile.

"Just stay on point at all times. Shit always seem to pop off when you least expect it too. Believe that!" Kilo admonished.

Rah Rah has been selling drugs for Kilo about six months now. Kilo took a liking to him because he was a sharp kid and extremely smart for his age. In a lot of ways he reminded Kilo of himself when he was young. He was smart, brave, and poor as hell.

Kilo pulled Rah Rah off of the block when he heard that he was running around with the wrong crowd, and robbing everybody. Kilo understood his story because he knew that Rah Rah's mother was a crack head. This was the same thing that Kilo and a lot of other hustlers in the hood had to go through. Kilo knew the young kid had nobody and plus he was thorough. The deadly combination of the two most of the time was all you needed to breed a real niggah. Recognizing his potential Kilo quickly pulled him on his team.

Kilo reached into the ashtray to retrieve a blunt he had rolled earlier. The blunt contained some of the best weed Rochester has seen in a while. He purchased it from the Jamaicans on the Strip. For some reason every winter they were able to flood the hood with it. Kilo put fire to the end of the long blunt and inhaled the smoke deep into his lungs. The unique smell of the loud quickly drew Rah Rah's attention. His lungs were yearning for a pull also.

Kilo sat in the dark living room smoking as he thought about Kiki. Her gorgeous eyes were the bomb. Her sexy ass full lips were as thick as Fantasia's. He inhaled more of the loud. 'She wants me to make her cry,' he thought with a smile. As soon as he blew out a cloud of smoke from his last pull, Rah Rah yelled, "Rollers!!" He had noticed the white van coming before it even stopped at the curb, and before the masked police began jumping out.

"Kilo the police is coming!!" he yelled again.

"Oh shit!" Kilo managed to say as he snapped back into reality. "Rah- grab that gun and run out of the back!" Kilo ordered as he stood to his feet and started grabbing the stacks of money off the table and stuffing it down his briefs. Without any real hesitation Rah Rah grabbed the shiny pistol from the table and began running towards the back of the house.

Kilo quickly snatched up the napkin that was holding the bags of crack and ran up the stairs while being sure to kill all the lights in his path. When he finally reached the bathroom he heard the first of a series of bangs from the police's battering ram. It sounded as if they were trying to knock the little house down.

Kilo ran to the toilet and plunged the napkin full of crack as far down the hole at the base of the toilet as he could. He nervously pulled on the lever as he released the napkin to be carried away. Remembering Snowman's two suspect twenty dollar bills, he pulled them from his pants pocket and flushed them also. He flushed the toilet two more times just to be sure that all of the evidence was gone. Kilo then ran out of the bathroom and into an adjacent upstairs bedroom. His heart was beating a thousand times a minute. He knew this was a serious situation. The RPD had already killed numerous black men in drug raids just like this one. He knew that they would have no problem killing again.

Kilo could hear the police downstairs flipping furniture over and yelling, "Police!"

One yelled, "We have one in the kitchen! Freeze!" Kilo then heard Rah Rah screaming to the top of his lungs.

Realizing that the blunt was still dangling from his lips Kilo began smoking to calm his nerves. He was lying on the floor behind the door of a dark room. He heard footsteps racing up the stairs. They were getting closer and closer. He pulled on the blunt harder and harder. The police yelled, "We know you're up here!"

Kilo took another long drag from his blunt and reluctantly yelled, "I'm in here!" He didn't want the police to be startled when they discovered him in the dark room and start firing. So he made the quick decision to announce where he was. "Don't shoot! I'm in here!"

"There's another one in the bedroom!" an officer shouted.

About four police officers rushed into the room. Kilo was lying face down with his hands already behind his back. The police had their guns drawn and their flashlights beaming into Kilo's face. He felt a painful kick to his mouth. Blood poured. Police started punching and kicking him from every angle. He couldn't see where the next blow would come from because of the bright lights. He felt the pain of every blow deep in his soul, but no matter where they hit him he never let out a sound.

After the beating they finally handcuffed and dragged Kilo back downstairs. The police were all over the house searching every crevice. Some of the officers wore masks and black shirts with the word **Police** written on the backs. The other officers were dressed in their regular blue uniforms.

The first thing Kilo noticed besides the entire living room being flipped upside down was Lil' Rah Rah sitting on the living room floor. Like his, Rah Rah's white shirt was covered with blood. He was sobbing like a little bitch. Not because he was in deep trouble, but because when the police caught him trying to squeeze out of the kitchen window they beat the shit out of him.

"You're going to jail tonight asshole!" a Sergeant said as he rushed up into Kilo's face. "We found the gun and we have a sell also."

Kilo laughed as he looked around to make eye contact with Rah Rah who wasn't crying as much now that Kilo was there, and said back to the Sergeant, "I don't give a fuck! I'll be home before the news gets back to the hood."

CHAPTER THREE
MURDERER

"As humans we are blessed with two natural abilities of God. We can create life which is a blessing. It is a fathers joy and a mothers delight to bring a child into this world. No matter how harsh or troublesome it is on earth. On the other hand, we have the ability to also take life. He who takes a life is automatically considered evil. He is cursed until his death. No matter how it happens and regardless of what the consequences are he will always be a murderer. Some men put this title on their chest, beat it with both hands, and chalk it up as being just a part of the game. Failing to realize that the dead were once the joy and delight of a mother and a father..."

Kiki waited by the window in her master bedroom that over looked the driveway. It had been more than two hours since she last talked to Kilo. He hadn't called and he was ignoring her phone calls. She didn't want to think that anything bad happened to him, but she felt in her heart that he would be so wrong to stand her up tonight.

When the phone rang she ran to it like the blue cordless phone that rested on her bed was Kilo himself. "Where are you!" she answered in an angry tone.

"Listen bitch. I have a pussy just like you do. So I know I don't have what your waiting for," her best friend Renee countered on the other line; two o'clock in the morning. "Pay attention to the caller ID bitch."

"What do you want Renee?" Kiki asked with a hint of frustration.

"You sound like you mad about something Kiki. I was going to ask for some money until I cash my check tomorrow. I need it to eat lunch with, but I'll call you back in the morning," Renee said backing off.

"No it's fine. You can stop by and get twenty dollars in the morning… I was just upset because Kilo was supposed to be home like two hours ago and I haven't heard from him yet," Kiki explained as she put the phone between her shoulder and ear, then began walking back over to the window.

"Kiki I've known you for almost ten years. I was there when you first got your period. You aren't only worried, you also horny as hell too! I can hear it all in your voice," Renee said as if she was a sex expert.

"Okay I may be a little horny, but you know I'm more concerned about my man."

"Something probably came up and he's out handling business. He'll be home to get you pregnant tonight," Renee said with a hysterical amount of laughter. She was the type of female that could find a joke to make about any serious situation.

"Shut up! I am not trying to get pregnant girl. You got mad jokes. Call me in the morning," Kiki said before she hung up on her friend.

Kiki slowly walked back to her huge king-sized bed. She crawled over the silk sheets and sat up against the gigantic pillows. She was wearing a pink set of see through bra and thongs made by Victoria's Secret. The bra revealed to the eye a perfect set of round nipples. Her pubic hair was neatly trimmed into the shape of an upside down triangle. It was easily visible through the front of her thongs.

Kiki wanted to surprise Kilo with some slow music and a cold bottle of Ciroc; which was his favorite drink. The alcohol was like a prerequisite before the hot passionate sex. She might need to be drunk if she planned on letting Kilo have his way with her tonight.

Kilo had taken her virginity years ago and to this day he was the only man to have made love to her. This was something Kiki was very proud about. Growing up in Marketview Heights she never wanted to be placed into the category of a whore or to have people in the hood calling her a slut. She also decided to stick with one guy because she didn't want to be a statistic.

Kiki was the epitome of a "good girl". She was smart, beautiful, and respectful. So much so that tonight she wanted to let go a little and give Kilo a chance to explore her wild side. This was the first time she ever wore a pair of thongs in her life. She couldn't wait to see the look on Kilo's face when he laid eyes on her long pecan legs. He would go crazy when he saw his sweet and innocent lady wearing the sexiest lingerie he'd ever seen. This outfit wasn't the main prize for Kilo tonight either. She also was planning to go down on him for the first time. This was something she vowed to save for their marriage, but tonight just felt so right.

Every man wanted a freak in the sheets and that's exactly how Kiki felt as she laid in bed. It wasn't a bad feeling. In fact she kind of liked it. The only thing missing was the presence of Kilo. She opened up the bottle of Ciroc and poured herself a drink. It was getting late and Kiki was growing tired. She placed her glass on the nightstand. After waiting for a long time she finally dozed off while fighting the urge of playing with her own moist womanhood.

— ‹(●)› —

"Tymer Miller!" the judge summoned.

Kilo walked into the courtroom being led by a tall white deputy who was holding his arm firmly. Kilo still had on his Ralph Lauren button up shirt and blue denim jeans. The only thing missing was his platinum jewelry. The deputy led him to the podium in front of the judge, and then he stood behind Kilo with his back to the entrance of the courtroom.

"Good morning Sir. Are you Tymer Miller?" the judge asked. She was a well-aged black woman who seemed to be very polite and intelligent.

"Yes your honor… I am," Kilo said as he leaned forward to speak into the microphone. Last night it was hard for him to sleep in the nasty holding cell of Central Bookings. Because he was charged with a felony it was mandatory that he spent the night in jail and wait until the following morning to see a judge for bail.

After Kilo answered the judge he looked over his shoulder and scanned the frustrated faces of the packed courtroom until he spotted Kiki in the second aisle. He also noticed her brother Cedric (Smooth C) and his right hand man Kay Cee seated next to her. Kilo was extremely happy to see that his people had shown up for court. Now all he needed was a bail and he could be out.

Pre-trial release called Keisha at 6:00 am to verify Kilo's information and address. She was furious when they informed her that Kilo had been arrested and charged with possession of a firearm and criminal sale of a controlled substance. 'He was supposed to be home with me,' she thought. 'How could he have been so careless?' The lady from pre-trial told Kiki that Kilo would be arraigned in city court at 9:00 am. She further explained that since Kilo had no previous criminal history that their office would do its best to get him released under their supervision.

Last night after taking a mug shot and being finger printed Kilo used his one phone call to contact Kay Cee. He explained to him that the police had busted the house and found a gun. He told Kay Cee to show up in court in the morning with at least ten grand for bail money. Even though it was his first time being in jail; the charges against him and the fact that he was a black man wrapped up in the criminal justice system could constitute a high ass bail.

"Sir the court demands your undivided attention. You are charged with some very serious crimes and I think it would be in your best interest to pay close attention. Do you understand Mr. Miller?" the judge asked wisely.

"Yes Ma'am," Kilo whispered into the microphone.

"Are you able to afford an attorney Sir?" asked the judge.

"I can afford a different lawyer for each charge if I have too," Kilo said boldly. Everyone sitting in the courtroom chuckled at his response, especially Keisha, Smooth C, and Kay Cee.

"Suit yourself Mr. Miller. You are being arraigned today for the charges of possession of an illegal firearm in the third degree, and also you are charged with criminal sale of a controlled substance in the second degree. These allegations allegedly taking place on or about December 14th at 73 Weld Street on the northeast side of the city. Do you understand these allegations against you Mr. Miller?"

"Yes I do your honor," Kilo said.

"And how do you plea?"

"Not guilty," Kilo answered confidently.

"Okay then, I'll enter in a plea of not guilty on your behalf. Mr. Thurgood would you like to be heard on this matter?" the judge asked as she turned her attention to the District Attorney who stood at the podium with Kilo.

"Sure. Thanks your Honor. I would like to note that in this case Mr. Miller has a co-defendant who is fifteen years old by the name of Rahmel Thomas. He's being held in the juvenile detention center. And in addition to the charges you've just read before the court and the defendant pertaining to this matter. Mr. Miller also has a warrant for murder in the second degree which dates back three years ago to 2011. Also allegedly taking place in the Marketview Heights area of the city of Rochester. People moves that the defendant be held in custody without bail until further proceedings," the District Attorney finished as he shot Kilo a wry smile that said without words, 'We got you now.'

There was a sudden commotion in the courtroom and this time it wasn't any laughter. Kiki fell onto her brother's shoulder as she cried uncontrollably. Kay Cee jumped up and shouted, "He didn't murder any fucking body. Someone's lying!" Two deputies' rushed over to escort Kay Cee out of the courtroom as he continued screaming and shouting for Kilo's innocence. Smooth C held his emotionally crushed sister in his arms as he waited to hear the rest of the judge's comments.

Kilo's heart sunk to the bottom of his body. He didn't know what to say or to think. He just stood motionless as more deputies formed around him. He couldn't believe they were charging him with a homicide so late afterwards. '*Are they serious?*' he thought. '*Who in the fuck could have told?*'

"Order in the courtroom! Outbursts like that will not be tolerated," the judge shouted as she continuously banged her gavel in front of her. There was a brief halt in the bedlam that erupted in the courtroom.

"From hearing the new charges I will hold the defendant without bail in the Monroe County Jail pending further proceedings. Keep in mind that the defendant is innocent until he is proven guilty. Court is dismissed!" she said before hammering her gavel once more.

CHAPTER FOUR
DEATH WISH

"Trials and tribulations will arise in a man's life especially when he's committed it to doing wrong. These often troublesome situations demand for an individual to use his mind in order to brainstorm ways of overcoming his ordeal. Some men are able to choose a righteous approach in order to save others from his burdens, but there are those whose affliction seems too harsh for them to bear alone. When the latter happens he feels no remorse for anyone. Only his prevailing is what's most important..."

With Kilo in jail Anne could now freely roam the Strip. Before, Kilo's presence had prevented her from hanging around in Marketview Heights. On many occasions Kilo was forced to drag his mother off of the block. He hated when she would come around with her corny ass jokes making a fool of herself. When Kilo was home Anne would have to send other crack heads to buy crack for her. She tried to the best of her ability to be a closet smoker. But it was hard to hide the fact that her body was slowly withering away because she was smoking that shit.

Now the third party wasn't necessary because her son was in jail for murder and the word on the streets was that he's never coming home. Besides Kilo, Anne also feared for her older brother

Freddie to catch her out in the streets. He always would preach to her about God punishing her for the sins she was committing and that she could be saved if she'd just turn her life over to Jesus. Anne couldn't see her life without being high on crack cocaine and even if what her brother preached about Jesus saving her was true, she just wasn't trying to hear it.

Freddie wasn't always the preacher friendly type of person he is now. Back in the days he was a pimp who protected his women with a gun if necessary. He was an original pimp. After a life altering event he gave his life over to God and retired from the game with the profits of a successful pimp. And with his luck he married a young Brazilian woman named, Lisa, who was an aspiring model.

On this particular day Anne strolled down the Strip peacefully. Her son wasn't around, nor did her brother pull up alongside of her in his cream Cadillac. She was in dire need of getting high, but she was also dead ass broke. Luckily she knew who to go to when she couldn't afford to pay for a bag of crack with cash.

Flames, he was known for buying sex from fiends in the hood. In fact, that's how he inherited his name. Everyone always joked that his dick had to be on fire after fucking so many crack heads, thus nicknaming him Flames. He knew that it was cool to buy fiend pussy if that was your thing, but tricking with Anne was forbidden. It was no secret that her son was a killer and everybody in the hood knew that. Flames knew that if Kilo ever found out about him fucking his mother it would be his death wish. '*Fuck that*,' Flame's thought. '*Kilo is about to go under the jail.*'

Flames promised Anne a dime bag of crack, and then he snuck her behind an old abandoned house. Since the crack epidemic prostitution had gotten extremely cheaper. It is widely believed among ghetto scholars that it was crack cocaine who put an end to the pimping game.

The two found a decent spot on the back porch of the house. Anne pulled her pants down to her ankles and laid face down on the concrete surface. Her face was pressed down in the midst of broken glass, piss, and God only knows what else. What was left of her once round ass was tooted up in the air as Flames gripped her waist with both of his hands and began pounding her from behind.

His actions was nothing more than lust, spite, hate and all of the other negative words to describe the way you feel for a man. This was violation number one. Anne was a washed up old lady. He had no business tricking with Kilo's mother in the first place, even if she was just a "crack head".

Flames ignored the toxic fumes that Anne's dry spot exhaled with every thrust. He was fucking her like she was the new girl on the block. "Lay all the way down. Yea, put that leg up a little," Flames directed. He let his body fall down on top of her back as he grinded deep inside of her pussy. Anne acted like it was good to her but being that she had already run through hundreds of men during her lifetime; he was really doing nothing.

"Hit this pussy harder. Oh yea, I like that!" Anne said as she pushed an old Sprite can away from her face.

Flames suddenly pulled out of her, and said, "Let me get some of that good head? You know how I like it Anne."

"You got to hurry up now baby. You didn't say you wanted both for just one bag," Anne complained as she stood up brushing the dirt off of the front of her shirt. All she could think about was getting a bag of crack and she knew pleasing Flames was the only way to get it without money.

Anne dropped to her knees and began giving him the best of her wet, sloppy, and toothless head until he exploded into her mouth.

⇒«◐»⇐

Kay Cee awoke to the sound of the ringing telephone, "Hello?" he whispered into the receiver.

"Good morning Kenny. You told me to call and remind you of your visit with Kilo today. It's eight o'clock and I scheduled the visit for ten o'clock," Kiki explained.

"Yea, Keisha I damn near forgot today was Monday. I went to the club last night, and I got drunk as hell... Do you want to come with me?" Kay Cee offered.

"Not today. I spoke to Kilo yesterday and he said that he needed to speak with you about something really important. So I'll stay home and let you boys visit alone this time. I'll go see him on Friday."

"Okay, but you meant to say men," Kay Cee corrected.

"Whatever you say Kenny I didn't mean any disrespect. Have a nice visit, and make sure you tell my baby I said I love him," Kiki asked.

"I will. And if you ever need anything let me know. The sky is the limit. Even if my boy doesn't pull through this one you know I'll always look out for you Keisha."

"Okay, I'll keep that in mind," Kiki said as they ended their brief conversation.

Kay Cee placed the phone back on its hook, and then wrapped his arm around Malinda's shoulders. She was sleeping on his bare chest. He had picked her up from S & T's night club which was located on the outskirts of Marketview Heights. Sunday nights usually pulled in at least three hundred people. Last night it might have exceeded its normal capacity because there were people crowded together inside from front to back. The deejay was playing all of the new hit songs, and the ladies were dancing like crazy.

Kay Cee had a slight hang over as a result of the numerous shots of Remy Martin he had consumed. The last hour of the club he winked at the club's owner and thus all drinks for the ladies were free. In that process of trying to keep up with them in drinking he must have took back ten straight shots of Remy.

S & T's was Kilo and Kay Cee's known hangout. They both were sure to represent for the hood when the two was in there because people from all over the city came out to party. It was their opportunity to show the whole city that they were major niggahs. Everything had changed in the last two months with Kilo in jail. Kay Cee no longer stood in the shadows of the more flamboyant Kilo. Now he was alone in the lime light and he enjoyed being the man for a change. Deep down inside he really did miss Kilo, but it sure did feel good filling his shoes when before all he could do was imagine how it felt to receive so much love.

During the short period of time Kilo has been gone. Kay Cee's money has swiftly increased. He easily managed to stack over $250,000 dollars, and began buying three kilograms of cocaine at a time from the Dominicans. Last week he walked onto the lot of a foreign car dealership and came away driving a money green Jaguar. He traded in his old gold chains and bought two platinum joints with iced out crosses that both hung down to his stomach.

Kay Cee was glowing in the hood. The ladies always flocked around the light-skinned pretty boy hustler. Kilo always would tell him that he had to be Rochester's biggest trick. It was no problem for Kay Cee to spend money on his women. He called it charity. The only real difference between Kilo and Kay Cee was their height and skin complexions. Kay Cee was light and short. Kilo was tall and brown-skinned, and they both had long braids. There really isn't too many more differences, but the streets have created over time a lot of similarities between the two soldiers.

Ever since they were small kids both of the two went to school and grew up together in Marketview Heights. They fought every fight on teams like brothers. Neither one had a brother by blood, but soon they created a bond similar to it. Kay Cee was a little older than Kilo and was the one to introduce him to selling drugs. Being that Kilo had the brains and the motive for getting money he perfected hustling as if it were an art. Whatever he said happened and once he tasted the fast money Kilo never looked back.

Whenever shit wasn't clicking right with their hustle and they were pressed for quick cash they would rob the local drug dealers in the hood. Back in those days Kilo would shoot niggahs for the simplest violations. If a victim wasn't moving fast enough or didn't get on the ground quick enough Kilo's gun was firing. Kay Cee always believed that Kilo was trying to get even in the hood for his sister getting murdered. There were a lot of different rumors about who was responsible, but for the most part Kimberly's death remained a mystery. Kay Cee never complained about Kilo being so trigger happy because they always came out of the robbery with one brick of cocaine here, $50,000 thousand there, and sometimes one fucked up hustler stretched out somewhere in the middle.

Kay Cee sat up in his king sized bed with his back pressed against the huge fluffy white pillows. He reached over and grabbed a clipped blunt from last night and relit it. He looked over at Malinda's half naked body as she rested next to him. She wasn't the prettiest woman in the world, but what her face lacked her sexy ass body definitely backed it up. Kay Cee knew that underneath the satin sheets she was naked. The shape of her round ass stood out calling him to caress it.

Malinda smelled the aroma of the burning weed and opened her eyes. Feeling her ass caused Kay Cee to remember how wet and good her pussy was last night. Malinda noticed Kay Cee's manhood rising and lifting up the sheets. She slid her hand under and began stroking him. The best thing about Malinda was her luscious full lips. It was the shiny red strawberry lip gloss that had truly gained Kay Cee's attention at the club. Wondering what she could do with them was partially the reason he decided to take her home.

Kay Cee pulled the sheets back off his lower body to reveal his erection that was in her soft grips. Malinda already knew what he expected next. Without needing a cue she bent her head down to meet his dick half way. Her soft lips smothered him as his head fell back onto the comforting pillows. It was no better feeling than a blunt and some early morning head simultaneously. Kay Cee gently stroked the back of her head with his left hand and smoked like a king with the other.

Kay Cee was running late for his visit with Kilo after he dropped Malinda off on the west side. It was a quarter past ten when he finally got to the jail and through the metal detectors. After a deputy frisked him and scanned his body with a hand held detector they buzzed him into the packed visiting room. He found his seat next to a Spanish female who was holding a newborn baby. Kay Cee looked around at the other visitors and their families. He spotted a few of his old chicks who were afraid to speak. He thought it was fucked up that they were in there kissing their men after what they had done to him sexually. Kay Cee made a mental note to keep an eye on Keisha while Kilo was in jail. He knew that it was the so-called innocent girls just like her that wind up being the sneakiest, 'and nastiest,' he thought.

After about ten long minutes Kilo finally came out wearing a beige jumpsuit with a pair of construction Timberlands on his feet. Kay Cee noticed how many females watched him as he swayed over show casing his natural swag, even from jail. Kay Cee excitedly stood up and gave Kilo a handshake that was followed by a brief hug. The two hadn't seen each other in two months and that was the longest separation they had ever experienced.

"What's going on Kay Cee? How are you?" Kilo asked as he sat down. There was a short piece of glass on the table that divided them.

"I'm good Kilo, but the important question is how you doing in here," Kay Cee said as he looked around the visiting room.

"My niggah, I'm peace. You know I'm a soldier. This jail shit could make or break a man, but I'll be damned if it gets the best of me. I do find myself stressing a lot, but I'm good for the most part. A niggahs just home sick that's all… I hear you out there shining son."

"Yea, you know this shit doesn't stop. You heard that I just pulled out the new Jag', right? I'm going to through some twenty fours on that bitch in the summer and kill these niggahs for real," Kay Cee bragged.

"No doubt fam'… But listen, you don't need the expensive ass cars. That shit only get niggahs like us crazy hot. Plus you already got that FED beef anyways," Kilo said referring to the drug and gun charges Kay Cee had pending.

"I hear what you saying, but a niggah only has one life to live. I have to shine. Fuck the police! This is the only car that I ever bought that really speaks about my hustle. Nobody's going to stop me from living the life that I deserve," Kay Cee said hoping he got his point across.

"Man shine by opening up a business or retiring from the game successful. Try giving back to our hood. Fuck flossing around in little ass Rochester! Kay Cee it's so many more sights to see. You should be able to see the big picture after witnessing so many nig-gahs before us go down on some bullshit. Hustlers that the hood looked up to got knocked, and now nobody even talks about them motherfuckahs anymore. Us, we already legends in the hood, but if we go to a club in Buffalo or Syracuse we become just two aver-age ass niggahs with chains and whips. The only love and respect we have comes from Marketview Heights. It's cool to be locally ac-cepted, but I really want to be internationally respected like a fuck-ing Jay-Z," Kilo said, and then pounded his fist on the table without drawing any attention from the Deputies.

"Man let me find out jail has you on some real Farrakhan shit. You still eat pork niggah?" Kay Cee said while crying laughing.

"I'm on some real smart shit now! I'm trying to beat this fucking case, and then come home to do major things. Like getting out of the hood like we always dreamed of," Kilo said demanding a seri-ous conversation. He stared across the table with a desperate look of needing Kay Cee's approval on this one. Shit has changed. He wore one of those expressions that only best friends could read, and Kay Cee saw it in his face that this murder case was really get-ting to him.

"Kilo, man don't worry… They don't have a fucking case! You hear me? I'll do whatever it takes to make sure that the morgue will have to drag a corpse into court to testify on you bra'. I swear to fucking God they will," Kay Cee said making it clear that he felt Kilo's pain and was willing to make it right by any means.

"And you know what Kay Cee? That's exactly what I needed to talk to you about today. That's why I told Kiki not to come with you because I knew it would get serious," Kilo said as he leaned closer to the dividing glass. "I just got my discovery packet from my lawyer last week. Your right they don't have shit. Just the bitch…"

"What bitch?" Kay Cee asked confused.

"Do you remember the niggah Rufus who used to live by the park? Tall brown-skinned dude that used to go to East High School with us," Kilo asked.

"Yea… yea. He has the sister with the fat ass and she used to drive a white Honda," Kay Cee replied.

"Her," Kilo said in a low disappointed voice. "The bitch told the police that she's positive it was me who shot the niggah Raheem. You should see her fucking statements. She's really telling Kay Cee."

Danasha Graham came forward to police about six months ago and claimed that while she was in the park with her son she saw Kilo shoot Raheem at close range. She said she observed an argument erupt near the basketball courts just before the shots were fired. Danasha said she saw Kilo with her own eyes pulling the trigger. The police put Kilo's picture in a six man photo array with five other men who resembled him, and within ten seconds, Danasha said, "That's him." She was pointing at Kilo. She further explained to police that the reason why she didn't report it to police earlier was because she feared for her life. Danasha said Kilo had "status" in the neighborhood and could easily have caused her harm. Not being able to live with her conscience was the underlying reason she decided to come forward now after three years. The police then took their time configuring a case against Tymer Miller, and soon a warrant was issued for his arrest.

"They gave me the bitches address and phone number in the discovery packet along with all of her statements. Make sure that her snitching ass will never be able to tell none of that shit to a jury," Kilo said, and then he passed his lawyer's business card over to Kay Cee with Danasha's information written on the back.

"Oh hell yea niggah she's finished. Her mother might as well prepare to buy her daughter a fucking coffin. Fuck trying to negotiate with her!" Kay Cee threatened.

The deputy stopped over to inform Kilo that his visit had expired and he kept walking. After they both shot the deputy with looks that could kill, they slowly stood up from their seats. When Kilo slapped hands with Kay Cee he cleverly took the balloon filled with weed from him. When nobody was looking he quickly swallowed it.

"Kay Cee be careful son. The system doesn't deserve to have both of us. One love. M.H. for life," Kilo said as he patted his fist against the left side of his chest. They both fought to hold back the tears that were wielding up.

"M.H. for life my niggah," Kay Cee said before he departed.

CHAPTER FIVE

FAITHFUL AND LOYALTY

"In order for a person to be successful he must truly understand the importance of choosing the right individuals to share his life with. Everybody needs trustworthy and supportive companions to help combat the harsh realities of this world. The people you allow in your circle are the ones who will watch your back or stab you in it. They will either do what you ask to help you or do what you didn't ask in order to harm you. He who comes to realize this truth has a better chance to overcome then he who strives at it alone..."

"Hi mother," Kiki said through the telephone as soon as she heard a hello.

"Hi baby, how are you doing?" her mother Diane asked excitedly when she recognized her daughters soft voice.

"I'm doing fine. I just finished cleaning up this house, and now I'm ready to get in my bed. I thought I'd call you to see if you were still going to church tomorrow," Kiki said.

"Of course I am darling. I wouldn't miss a day with the Lord even if my life depended on it."

"Alright so I'll pick you up around nine o'clock in the morning. Where's Cedric's big headed self at?" Kiki asked referring to her brother Smooth C.

"Child you know that boy is somewhere up on that corner. I tell him every day to stop messing around with them no good hoodlums. Cedric is going to get himself in a whole lot of trouble one day. Your mother is getting too old to be running behind you children like I used too," Diane said.

Smooth C was eighteen years old and just a few years younger than Keisha. He was a small time drug dealer who made his money by selling dime bags of crack in Marketview Heights. The majority of the money he made was spent on clothes, jewelry, and old year 2000 Acura and Honda's. Kilo made sure that he was always straight on the strength of his sister, but was kind of leery about really putting him on because Smooth C failed to show that he was ready to be a major niggah in the game. However, since Kilo has been in jail Smooth C has started to take hustling a little more serious than before. The handsome dark-skinned pretty boy has been putting the young girls on hold lately and focusing more on stacking his money.

"Mother please, you are not getting old. Age is just a number. It's all about how you feel that really matters," Kiki laughed.

"Girl I went to the doctor's office Monday and Mrs. Smith told me that my blood pressure was sky high," Diane exaggerated.

"Well Momma you need to start watching what you eat, and stay away from that butter and salt that I know you love. Start drinking lots of water too… Are you still exercising like Mrs. Smith told you?" Kiki asked in a concerned voice.

"Yes I get on the bike once in a while, but that only helps so much… So how is school coming along? And how is Tymer doing?" she asked quickly changing the subject.

"School is fine, and Tymer is doing well also. I'm going to see him on Monday."

"That sounds good to hear Keisha… So baby… you haven't been thinking about moving on yet? You know that boy is facing a lot of time and there's nothing wrong with you having friends until something becomes serious. I sure hate to say it, but it doesn't look good for Tymer if what the paper says is true."

"Please! It's only been three months and I have faith that he's coming home. Don't listen to what they say in the newspaper. They only print one side of the story, and that's normally the one that makes the accused look the worse. I believe in destiny and if it's not worth waiting for, then to me it isn't worth anything at all," Kiki said with dignity. "Besides I love Kilo to death. He's been good to me, and he's always been there when any of us needed him. So mother I intend on sticking by his side. I'm not one of these simple minded girls who leave a good man they claimed to love as soon as he gets into a bad situation."

"I understand Keisha, but I just want the best for my daughter. If you're happy, then Momma is happy too. Pray and God will make a way."

Diane did love Kilo. She watched him grow up from a little boy into a man. She always treated Kilo like her son. She just didn't want her daughter to get hurt if worse actually came to worse. Diane heard about the young man (Raheem) who was shot in the face at the park a few years ago. It happened right up the street from her house. She thought that it was a terrible thing the way young black men were killing each other in Rochester. She went to church the following Sunday after Raheem was murdered and prayed that the savage responsible would be brought to justice. Since then she had forgotten about the homicide until Keisha called, crying, with the news. Diane would have never believed Kilo was responsible for that heinous crime. She was under the impression that he had grown to be a fine young man with of course the minor flaw of being a drug dealer. But no matter the outcome she still wished the best for him and Keisha.

"I am happy mother. I appreciate your concern. We'll talk more in the morning. I love you," Kiki said.

"I love you too baby, good night."

He had been following her around everywhere she went for two days straight. She had inadvertently taken him all over the city of Rochester. Yesterday she went to the Greece Town Mall and stayed inside for three hours. When she came out she was carrying four bags from Macy's. Later that night he followed her to what appeared to be her mother's house on the Westside of the city. He figured the gray haired lady with glasses who came out onto the porch was her mother. Danasha and her son said goodbye by waiving to her before leaving. Early this morning a tall-dark skinned dude came to her house driving a black .745 BMW to pick up her son. The little boy looked like he was on his way to school because he had a book bag on his shoulders.

At about 4:00 o'clock in the afternoon she came out of her house wearing a waist length Ed Hardy jacket and a pair of tight dark blue jeans. Her ass was still round and fat like it was years ago when she lived in Marketview Heights. She had a pretty ebony face and wore her hair done in neatly braided micros tied up into a ponytail. After all these years she was still looking beautiful as hell. Kay Cee watched as her well-shaped ass bounced from side to side on the way to her car, which was parked at the curb just in front of her home on Dewey Avenue. She was driving a white Ford Focus.

Kay Cee cranked up the all black Chevy Impala that he was driving, and sped off behind Danasha as she pulled away from the curb. The extra dark tinted windows made Kay Cee feel almost invisible. Danasha was so caught up in making her moves that she never noticed she was being tailed all of this time.

Kay Cee loved the fact that she was a fast driver because it added a little more thrill to the chase, which at the right moment would have to come to a bloody end. Kay Cee thought, '*This cute little bitch could be doing something else with her life other than trying to send a good niggah like Kilo upstate forever.*' He could tell by her style that Danasha was still kind of young. '*She should have her young ass somewhere modeling.*'

Danasha breezed through a yellow traffic light that caught Kay

Cee on red. When the light turned green he pushed the Impala red line until she was back in sight. Kay Cee was trailing a few cars behind when he noticed Danasha was signaling right to get onto the expressway. "Where the fuck is she going?" Kay Cee asked out loud. It was fun weaving in and out of traffic while listening to Mobb Deep's old classic, *Murda Musik*. He was trying hard to keep her in his eye sight while traveling at high speeds.

Danasha was cruising in the direction of Buffalo, New York via I490 West. It was now about 5:30 pm and due to the winter season the sun was beginning to set. They'd been driving at seventy plus mph for quite a while now. Kay Cee had to flip on his windshield wipers to wash away the thick snowflakes that began to fall.

Kay Cee was singing along to one of Mobb Deep's catchy hooks when he noticed Danasha making a quick right into the parking lot of a small 'Quick Stop' motel. Kay Cee slowed down, and turned left into a Sonoco gas station that was across the expressway. He made sure to park in an empty space facing the motel.

Danasha got out of her car and walked inside of the motels main office. Kay Cee could see every room door clearly from his spot at the gas station. The snow continued to fall as he patiently waited to see what she would do next.

Kay Cee noticed the door to the office open, but he leaned back in his seat when he saw a white couple come out holding hands. They walked four doors down and used a key card to get into the room. Ten minutes later Danasha came out looking around the parking lot as she walked along the sidewalk. She seemed to be expecting someone. She came to the seventh door, slid her key in the lock, and went inside. When she closed the door behind herself, Kay Cee noticed a light come on in the room. He thought, '*Why in the hell would she come way out here to get a hotel room?*'

Almost an hour passed by and Danasha still was alone in the motel room. Kay Cee was on his cell phone talking to his Dominican cocaine suppliers, "Papi, Papi. Me gonna' need *two* plates of yellow rice and beans," he said into his phone. He was paying no attention to the red Toyota Camry that just pulled into the motel's parking lot.

"No problem. You come to the restaurant. I cook for you right now. Okay?" the Spanish voice said.

"Okay," Kay Cee said, and touched end call. "Oh shit! I know that isn't the bitch ass niggah Rondell from the town," Kay Cee said out loud as he turned down his music. He was willing to bet that he was coming to see Danasha.

Kay Cee leaned over the steering wheel as he watched Rondell walk up to the same door Danasha went into. Rondell was a broke nobody from the Westside of the R.O.C. They used to be in rival gangs back in high school. Kilo shot Rondell's older brother Marcus in the stomach back in the days.

Kay Cee watched the two hug and kiss in the doorway before the door closed behind Rondell.

'I knew this bitch was up to no good. I have a snitching ass bitch and a coward ass niggah in the same nest. I'm going to kill two birds with one bullet,' Kay Cee thought.

Kay Cee picked up a long, chrome .357 caliber handgun with a black rubber grip handle that was resting quietly on the passenger's seat. This same gun had been riding shotgun with him for two days; waiting patiently to be fired. Kay Cee felt bad for having to murder a female, but he knew that Kilo would do the same for him. Besides she didn't deserve any sympathy anyways. Danasha was from the hood. She knew it was rough in Marketview Heights and only the strong survived. She was aware of the fact that snitches got fucked up for running to the cops about serious shit like murder. That rule applied to every ghetto across America. Rondell, he was just in the wrong place at the wrong time, and fucking around with the wrong broad. Surely he'd pay for it with his life because he sure as hell wasn't going back to the R.O.C alive.

Kay Cee squeezed the gun into his coat pocket, started up the car, and drove across the expressway into the motel's parking lot. The snow was falling heavier now. You could barely see your hand if you held it up to your face. He found a parking space a few doors down from where Danasha and Rondell were. Kay Cee lifted the big hood that was trimmed with brown fur over his head, pulled the draw strings to conceal most of his face, and then he stepped out into the cold parking lot leaving the car running.

As he approached door number seven Kay Cee noticed that the light was off inside the room. He gripped the deadly .357 with his right hand. With his finger on the trigger he took a deep breath and started to knock on the door until he heard a male's voice answer.

"Who in the fuck is that?" Rondell shouted from the edge of the bed. He had one hand on the back of Danasha's head while she was on her knees sucking his dick to the beat of an Alicia Key's slow jam playing in the background.

"Room service," Kay Cee said in a muffled voice.

"We didn't call for any fucking room service!" Rondell screamed again.

"I'm sorry, but there's some sort of problem. You need to come to the door," Kay Cee explained in the same voice.

"Damn! Hold on," Rondell yelled to the door.

Rondell reluctantly pulled out of Danasha's mouth. "Hold on baby. Let me see what in the fuck they bothering us for." He put on a yellow hotel robe, while she climbed into the bed and underneath the sheets. When Rondell angrily snatched open the door he was met by the huge barrow of a .357. Kay Cee quickly grabbed a hold of his throat, and whispered, "Niggah don't say shit. I swear to God I'll blow your fucking brains out. Back the fuck in and don't say shit you stupid ass niggah."

Danasha was so shocked she couldn't even scream. All she could do was stare blankly at the huge gun in the stranger's hand. She silently watched Kay Cee push Rondell onto the bed while he closed the door and locked it. Neither Rondell nor Danasha knew what was happening.

"Get up bitch and stand next to the bed," Kay Cee directed Danasha by pointing his gun her way. "Leave the sheets on the bed. You have nothing to hide."

"I have a son. Please don't kill me. Whatever it is you want you can have. My money is in the purse," Danasha pleaded.

"Shut the fuck up. The next one to say a word will be the first one to die, understood?" Kay Cee asked as he pointed his gun at both of them. Their quick head motioning indicated a yes.

Kay Cee scanned the room as he kept his gun pointed at the frightened couple. There were five candles burning around the room, and the lovely scent of women's Faraway filled the corners of the room. Kay Cee couldn't help but to let his eyes explore Danasha's thick thighs and hairy bush of pubic hairs while she stood next to the bed completely naked. Kay Cee walked over to the bathroom to see if it had any windows. He then ordered Rondell to stand in there after he was positive he wouldn't be able to escape.

After Kay Cee slammed the door on Rondell, he took his hood and coat off revealing his identity to his hostage. Danasha immediately recognized him as being Kilo's roll dog from Marketview Heights, but was terrified to speak. Now she really feared for her life because she knew why Kay Cee was there, and what he came to do.

"Listen Danasha, I know you from back in the days. You are alright with me. I really don't want to kill you or your punk ass friend in there. So, if you'd just cooperate we could settle and leave this shit right here. Nobody will ever have to know about this okay?" Kay Cee asked in a friendly tone.

"Why did you follow me here? That's my word I wasn't going to court and testify on your friend. Niggahs paid me to tell on him. I used to have a crush on Kilo back then. I really needed the money, but I wasn't going to let him get convicted by me going to trial. I swear I wasn't!" Danasha pleaded as she covered each breast with her hands.

"Look I believe you. But for all of the trouble you've caused my man and his family I need a favor. All you have to do is give me some head and a shot of pussy, and then we can call it even," Kay Cee said while pulling out a condom from his pants pocket.

"Is that all you want? Then we can go separate ways?" she asked desperately. Danasha was confused as to why he only wanted his dick sucked and some pussy for all of the trouble she'd caused. Even with her doubts, she knew it was a request she couldn't refuse if she wanted a chance to live.

"We can go our separate ways," Kay Cee confirmed.

Kay Cee pulled his pants down just around his thighs and stretched his dick out through the hole in his boxers. When he walked over to her she dropped down to her knees with tears running down her cheeks. She grabbed a hold of his dick, looked him in his eyes, and started sucking and licking all over it. All the while he held his .357 clutched in his hand pointing at her temple. Kay Cee thought, '*It would be fucked up to die sucking the niggah who killed you dick.*'

"Get on the edge of the bed so I can fuck you from the back," Kay Cee ordered.

Danasha deep throated him once more before she complied. She climbed up on the bed and buried her face in the sheets causing her ass to spread behind her. Kay Cee ripped open the condom wrapper with his teeth, and then stood behind her as he pulled the latex on. Kay Cee slid the cold barrow of the gun along her wet womanhood. When she looked to see what he was doing, he flashed her with a smile. He entered her and was amazed at the tightness of her vagina. It felt so good to be inside of something so warm and inviting. He gripped her waist and pounded as hard as he could. She could feel the cold gun along her side.

Rondell had his ear to the bathroom door listening the whole time. He couldn't hear the conversation they had, but definitely could hear Danasha moaning and screaming as the bed rapidly knocked against the wall. "This bitch's baby father is crazy," he mumbled.

Danasha must have forgotten that she was being raped, and the niggah fucking her was taking her pussy at gun point. She began vigorously shaking her ass around in circular motions to meet Kay Cee's every thrust. She did this until she felt cum running down the insides of her thighs after her second time climaxing. Kay Cee switched to hard and long thrusts before he came also. He left the condom on and pulled up his pants.

Kay Cee walked over to the couch and put back on his coat and hood. Danasha was sitting on the bed licking her lips watching Kay Cee zip up his coat. The candle lights reflected off of her sweaty, caramel body. *'Damn he has some good dick,'* she thought.

"So who paid you to go to the police?" Kay Cee asked.

"Marvin. He gave me two thousand dollars and promised me another three grand after trial. But you know he's dead now anyways. I'll be stupid to go to trial knowing I wouldn't get shit from him."

Everybody in Marketview Heights knew of Marvin. He was making a lot of money selling weed a couple of years ago. He was kind of salty because Kilo was fucking his baby momma, Moesha. Marvin was at the dice game when Raheem was killed. So when he found out about Kilo and Moesha, instead of respecting the game, he paid Danasha to go to the police almost three years after the homicide. Unfortunately, two months ago Marvin was murdered in a robbery attempt to get him for his weed. The word in the hood is that when he resisted the stick-up, niggahs emptied a clip on his head alone, and then left him for dead in an apartment building.

"Danasha go open up that bathroom door for me. I want to let this coward ass niggah know that you just saved his life with your honesty, and your great pussy," Kay Cee said with the .357 clutched in his hand threatening the floor.

Danasha slowly got off the bed and walked towards the bathroom. She was no longer trying to hide her nakedness as she now let her breast hang freely. She thought everything was cool since she had told the truth about why she went to the cops; plus she had done as Kay Cee requested and he even complimented her sex.

"So can I see you again sometime… Kay Cee, right? At first I was shook when you came in here, but after you fucked me like that I like you now. And your right this niggah in here is a bitch," she said pointing to the door she was about to open.

"Definitely," Kay Cee said as he followed close behind her. He watched as her ass cheeks lifted up one at a time with each of her steps. He reached out and palmed her ass one last time. It was so soft and he was glad he decided to sex her when all he was sup- posed to do was put a bullet in her fucking head for snitching.

When Danasha twisted the knob and opened the door Kay Cee drop-kicked her in the back sending her flying into the bath- room. She let out a loud scream of pain before she landed on top of Rondell who was now seated on the toilet seat. His eyes grew wide when he saw Kay Cee step up and fire one shot into the screaming woman's back (Boom!). The next bullet from the chamber caught Rondell square in his bird chest (Boom!). They both died immedi- ately from their gunshot wounds. Danasha was slumped over with her head buried between Rondell's legs.

Kay Cee grabbed the draw strings to his hood, and fled the scene of a double homicide that was all in the name of Kilo.

CHAPTER SIX

PLEASE FATHER

"There are some who believe in a higher power of being besides man. Some people really believe in a God, but they've experienced so many bad times that they question the existence of an all-powerful being responsible for keeping them safe from harm. When things are going well there doesn't seem to be a need to make a connection with the spiritual part of life. Only when times are tough, and crises arise in your life is when you feel that a force greater than yourself is needed to overcome. Then you will submit to your rebellious nature and call on God for deliverance…"

Keisha awoke early in the morning to get ready for school. After she took care of washing her face and brushing her teeth she went downstairs to prepare herself a breakfast. As she walked into the kitchen the living room phone rang. She walked over and answered with a pleasant, "Hello?"

Renee yelled at her through the phone.

"Okay. Damn what happened?" Kiki asked as she quickly grabbed the remote control and dialed 1-0. She immediately saw the words 'Double Homicide' on the right corner of the screen. Her heart pounded as she thought of her brother Cedric somehow being involved. She silently held the phone to her ear as she watched and listened intently.

"We now bring you breaking news. A Rochester couple was murdered last night in a small motel just outside of the city of Buffalo. Twenty-six year old Danasha Graham and twenty-four year old Rondell Wilson were each killed by a single gunshot wound. The motel manager says that the female victim rented the room alone at approximately six forty-five pm. He was unaware of how and when the male victim arrived," the black Anchorwoman reported. They went on to show separate pictures of Danasha and Rondell on the screen, then live footage of police and investigators walking in and out of the motel room.

The Anchorwoman continued, "Apparently, both victims were found dead in the motel's bathroom by police around nine-thirty pm. As of right now police have no motive for the shootings, but they do tell us that Danasha Graham was a key witness in an upcoming murder trial here in Rochester. Police aren't sure if that in itself was related to yesterday's homicides. Witnesses next door reported hearing shots fired, but was unable to identify any suspects or get away vehicles. We will be sure to bring you more on this terrible and unfortunate story as it unfolds."

"Girl I was getting Jayquan ready for school this morning and I happened to turn to the news and I knew that girl's face looked familiar. She used to live in Marketview Heights with us right?" Renee asked.

"Yes. When Kilo was telling me about her I couldn't picture the girls face, but now I know exactly who she is. She was kind of cool back then too. I wonder if Kilo heard about this yet." Kiki asked as she wondered if Danasha's death would be good or bad news for her man.

"Hell yea! In jail those niggahs know everything. When Terrance was locked up I couldn't keep shit on the low from his ass. He found out about every niggah I was creeping with somehow," Renee explained.

"So is this good or bad for Kilo? Do you think he could come home because of this Renee?"

"Of course he could. I know a lot of dudes who got arrested for some serious shit, but they was let go because nobody came to court to testify on them. And God forgive me but it doesn't look like home girl will be making any court dates any time soon," Renee said.

"Renee if your not doing anything later come to my house. I'm about to call my mother and see what she says. She knows a little about the law. Damn I hope this boy could get out!" Kiki said as she disconnected with her friend.

Kiki dropped down to her knees in the middle of the living room floor and began a silent prayer, "Lord please! I'm calling on you God. Please make a way for Kilo to come home. I love him so much. He's not a bad person and I know from this that he's learned his lesson. Lord I'm like a dead soldier without him," she prayed. Tears rolled down her beautiful face. "Please Father I'm begging you!"

>(()(

Kilo awoke early in the morning thinking about the past and future of his life as he lay in his uncomfortable bunk. The terrifying thoughts of never seeing the streets again had caused him to toss and turn in his sleep all night. Nightmare after nightmare would send him rising out of his bed in cold sweats. He dreamed of images when Kiki was making love to other men. He had dreams of him dying in the streets, but he always woke up to the cold, lonely cell of the County Jail.

This morning Kilo didn't bother to get up for breakfast. He chose to stay locked in his empty cell on the meanest floor of the entire jail. The inmates long ago nicknamed his cellblock the 'House of Pain'. Once you walked in it felt as though you've just entered a steal caged match with some of the wildest niggahs Rochester mean streets had in store. If you weren't able to hold your own, then you were subject to feeling the pain during your entire stay in the

Monroe County Jail.

Some so-called "gangsters" were brought to the front of this cell block, and once they saw the mean faces of the men they'd be forced to share living space with they literally begged the deputy not to put them in there. Sometimes you'd get an asshole deputy and he'd toss you in with the wolves anyways, and after showing that sign of weakness, fear, you'd probably have to wash niggahs drawers in the slop sink. A real coward would be put under the wing of someone who was holding it down in the jail, and he'd only protect you in order to spend all your money on commissary to buy the things he liked or he'll run your girls phone bill up sky high by using her three-way calls. Somehow you were sure to pay in one way, shape, form, or fashion.

In many inmates' opinion the County Jail was worse than being sent to prison Upstate. It was rough, but if you were a respectable figure in the streets you'd be alright in any jail because real always recognizes real. The House of Pain housed the predators and the prey was devoured. Kilo stood among the elite because he was a real street figure whose name rung bells outside of jail. On the outside he was known for shooting niggahs and getting money. Thus, nobody wanted problems with him.

Kilo had run into a couple minor problems since he'd been locked up. One incident happened when he first came in. He knocked out this kid from the South Side because he stepped on his brand new Timberlands. It was petty, but when you just came back from court and had been charged with murder everything was to be taken seriously. Plus Kilo wanted to make an example out of his ass anyways because he was the loudest talking niggah on the cell block. Kilo hit old boy with two quick punches; an upper-cut that landed on the bottom of his chin and a short right hook to the side of his jaw. Blood flew everywhere as the kid fell up under the table unconscious to the world. Later on that night the kid came over to Kilo's cell with a black eye to ask Kilo if he needed any of his boxers washed.

The other fight Kilo had occurred last week in the gym. Some big black dude punched Kilo in his face right before he could lay the basketball in the hoop. While they were fighting the dude kept yelling, "This niggah killed my cousin...Bitch ass niggah you killed Raheem!" That fight didn't last long before almost six niggahs from Marketview Heights ran over and put his ass to sleep. Kilo jumped on Raheem cousin's face several times before the deputies came running, spraying mace into the crowd, and finally tackling Kilo hard to the wooden floor.

Kilo finally rose up, and then out of the hard bunk in his small cell. He stood up and stretched a few times before walking over to the filthy toilet in the corner to take a piss. The television was in the front of the cell block and he could only hear the claps and chants of, "Jerry, Jerry!" One thing that he really hated about his cell was the fact that he was blind to the television whenever he was locked in.

Kilo sat back down on his cot, and eyed the Bible that was resting on the gray commissary box in front of him. An old timer gave it to him two months ago before he was released. He came to know Kilo by playing chess with him. The O. G told Kilo that chess was the game of life, but only God directs the moves. "You may put the opponent into checkmate Kilo, but only if God gives you the wisdom to do so. Receiving this divine wisdom from God is a dangerous thing because it makes you responsible for your future actions. God can get you out of this situation Kilo, but if you return to the same house you left your troubles will be seven times greater than before," O. G had explained over their final game of chess.

Kilo had never been a religious person. The events of his life forced him to question God every time something bad happened to him, except for this time. Kilo curiously took the Bible from O. G and read it every day. He bought a pair of black rosary beads from commissary, and then started going to church services held in the gym every Sunday. He believed in God more now than he ever did before.

Kilo stood at the front of his cell with his arms extended out through the bars as he watched the other inmates walk back and forth on the cell block. He noticed Mark walking towards him holding a newspaper.

"Kilo man you need to read this shit they have in the paper about your case!" he said with a big ass smile as he handed the paper over to Kilo.

"What are they saying now?" Kilo asked. The newspaper has been printing different shit about him every time he went to court.

Kilo pulled the newspaper into his cell and read the front headline: Witness in Murder Trial Slain in Buffalo, New York. Kilo then read through the story of Danasha and Rondell being murdered at a motel. He knew that Kay Cee was responsible for their deaths. He understood that they were killed so that he could possibly be freed. Kilo wondered how many people in the world were willing to do this for a friend.

"So what does this mean for your case Kilo? You're going home, huh?" Mark asked as he took the paper back.

"Hopefully," Kilo replied with a mild smirk.

"Shit I hope so son. You are too cool to be stuck in jail," Mark said before he walked off.

Kilo picked up his Bible, and then lowered himself to his knees. With his elbows on the edge of the bed and his hands clasped in front of his face, Kilo began in prayer, "Father I pray to you today. I once again ask for forgiveness in Jesus' name. In my short life I have been through a lot of pain. My mother is addicted to crack cocaine. I lost my baby sister at a young age. Of course you already know these things, but I'm just trying to understand how I got to be who I am. Besides losing my freedom; I lost the one person that ever really loved me, Keisha. Lord faced with life behind these bars I have not questioned you in no way. Like Job I hold fast to my faith. I have turned to you to save me from destruction. I can't honestly say that if you save me from this situation that I'll be out of the streets for good, but I could say that I'll be a good person and inspire to leave the streets one day soon."

Tears fell from Kilo's eyes as he continued in prayer ignoring the inmates who were walking past. "Father hear me, please! I am who I am. I'm a product of my environment, but I am also a child of yours. Give me another chance to be able to hold Keisha again. She is a good woman who deserves to be loved."

Kilo looked up at the ceiling of his cell as tears continued to flow from his eyes and said, "Lord, I am begging you. Amen."

CHAPTER SEVEN
THEY DON'T LIVE LONG

"The way a person decides to live their life in the long run will determine if he/or she keeps it. Premature death is a hurtful feeling for the deceased family members, but the way that the dead person lived will tell whether the particular death will be felt. A man or woman who walks the earth with integrity and respect for self and mankind will be wished well at their burial, but if he/or she lived with certain unacceptable corruption then they may not be missed at all..."

Anne had been spending her companies' money on crack since early yesterday afternoon. The fat white man with an extremely pointy nose and round glasses came into the city of Rochester from one of the many surrounding suburbs in search for crack cocaine. With his luck as he slowly rode through Marketview Heights obviously looking to get high he was flagged down by a desperate Anne.

After taking him to Flames to buy ten bags of cocaine, she then took him back to her filthy one bedroom apartment. Her bed was in the middle of the living room and only consisted of two pissy mattresses stacked up on top of each other. Her refrigerator looked like a Christmas tree with no decorations. It hasn't seen any food since she moved in two years ago. Anne had reached the point in her life to where nothing mattered anymore except getting high.

Nowhere in the desolate apartment has seen more action than those two mattresses. Anne had long ago knocked the springs in them loose while turning tricks.

The fat weird looking white man was completely naked as he lay across the bed. His legs were spread apart with Anne between them sucking on his puny dick like it was a well filled with riches. The white man's eyes were open wide as they possibly could as he enjoyed the best of both worlds. He held his hot stem to his mouth and inhaled the crack smoke deep into his lungs, while Anne was swallowing him.

Anne noticed while she was sucking his dick that his pants were on the floor right next to the bed. He had been supplying her with crack, but she wasn't interested in the sexual part. She reasoned that if she could get the rest of his money she could continue to get high, but alone. She got up onto her knees in front of him and began to caress her aged breasts. She reached out and took the hot stem from the white man who seemed to be zoned out into another world. After Anne took a hit of what was left in the glass dick she said, "Bob I bet your wife never sucked it like that. I told you Momma was going to take good care of you, huh?"

Bob didn't respond he just continued to stare at the ceiling.

"I want some more of your tongue. You want to eat Momma's pussy again?" she asked. With a slow up and down head motion, Bob agreed.

Bob was so high he didn't know what in the hell she was saying or which one of her was doing the talking. He was so spaced out that he was seeing three of her in front of him. Noticing Bob's current state of ignorance Anne tugged at his ankles and slid his body down on the bed some. She purposely placed the stem on the floor next to Bob's pants before she crawled over his pale white body and mounted his face. Anne stripped his glasses off figuring it'll be a bright idea to further impair his vision. Once Bob tasted her sour juices he wasted no time before he went to work on Anne's clit as she grinded wildly on his mouth. Anne bent over with Bob's glasses in hand. Once she dropped them to the floor she pulled his pants closer to the bed.

Anne rode Bob's face like a champion for ten minutes. She began faking an orgasm by wildly gyrated her pussy over Bob's face. He licked and sucked when he could. At the first chance Anne bent to the side and reached into the first pocket available on Bob's pants. Bingo. She pulled out a hand full of crisp twenties. They felt like they were fresh from the bank. She clutched them in her hand tightly as she finished riding her victims face. After smearing the foul fluids from her pussy all over Bob's face, she quickly rolled off of him.

Anne grabbed her dingy gray sweatpants and her black bra, and then sprinted into the bathroom. Once she safely got inside she hurried and put on her clothes. The excitement had spoiled her high. She nervously counted the green twenty dollar bills with a wide smile. To her surprise she had pulled a hundred and forty dollars from Bob's pocket. Now all she had to do was try to get rid of his dumb ass.

Bob sat up and wiped his face dry with both of his hands. After he retrieved his glasses from the side of the bed he realized that they'd smoked the last of the crack, and he wanted to send Anne to get some more.

Bob worked at a major construction company twenty miles from Rochester. He spent one weekend a month in the city smoking crack and paying to get laid. Tonight was his last night out before he had to get back home to his wife and three children, plus be back to work early Monday morning. He reached and grabbed his pants to count the rest of his money, but was confused when he stuck his huge hand into four empty pockets.

"Motherfuckah' get the hell out of my house you white son of a bitch… get the fuck out!" Anne yelled as she came bursting out of the bathroom exhibiting one of the oldest fiend routines in the book. "Oh- no cracker… nobody plays me. I'll call the police if you don't get the fuck out of my house!"

Anne continued yelling all kinds of curses towards Bob as she knocked over furniture and began throwing beer bottles against the wall.

Bob was too angry about his missing money to be startled by her sudden rage. Usually this stunt would work on the average cowardly white person visiting Marketview Heights, but in this case the gigantic white man lunged up from the bed and clasped his mighty hands around Anne's throat.

"Where's my money? You black whore I want my fucking money!" he shouted.

His face turned as red as the devil himself while choking Anne viciously. "I want my money!" he demanded.

Anne tried to grab a hold of his massive forearms in an attempt to struggle. She kicked, punched, and scratched desperately wanting to be freed. But everything she tried only made him more furious as he tightened his grip around her neck. If he wasn't so high, he probably would have noticed her face turning blue. Had it not been for the effects of crack cocaine he could have seen her bloodshot red eyes popping out of her sockets. If he wasn't so high maybe he would have felt the struggle end and the last of Anne's spirit ascending from her dead body…

Federal agents Mike Ledgeworth and Benny Thompson had been investigating their own informant for two months now. The notorious drug dealer had been a cooperating fink for about a year since he was caught in possession of illegal drugs and a firearm. He told on his best friends, and he didn't hesitate to snitch on his enemies and competition. It was hard for the agents to get him to flip, but after hearing the outrageous amount of time he was facing behind bars he became more than willing to help his white rivals in their fight against crime.

Although agent Benny Thompson was a black man with heavy

dark skin he would fool anybody into believing that he was a white man; trapped inside a black body. He truly hated his own black flesh with a passion. What he hated most however was a mixed or light-skinned person. He didn't know if he was supposed to love your lightness or despise your ethnicity. Benny Thompson was a fucked up person, and it showed in his work. On the other hand, Mike Ledgeworth was the nice guy. He was the one who always convinced the weak minded hustlers to tell everything they knew by using his wit. Benny only relied on intimidation and it sometimes worked like a charm.

Even though their best and most productive rat in terms of arrests did a great deal of cooperating he was beginning to make too much money selling drugs while dodging prosecution. The information he has been providing lately was weak and rarely led to major arrests. The deal was that he help bring down his major connections of crack suppliers, and in return he could stay free and successfully rise to the top of the Rochester drug trade. The agents painted a pretty picture in his head of him standing alone on top of a crack cocaine mountain. He should have known that cops were never to be trusted in this game. A true niggah to the streets will take the jail sentence before losing his soul and destroying his reputation as a hustler.

Since he began cooperating with the likes of Mike Ledgeworth and Benny Thompson he has been literally getting away with murder. Once the agents found out about the deaths of Danasha Graham and Rondell Wilson they instantly decided to renege on their promises after discovering the connection between the double homicide and the murder case of Tymer Miller. They believed that their informant Kenny Conway and the close friend of Mr. Miller were involved in the shooting death of his friend's key witness. Once they were able to compile enough evidence linking Kenny Conway to the murders they'd bring him in with an ultimatum. Either he wore wires to perform hand to hand sells with known drug dealers from now on or he would spend the rest of his life in prison. And the only reason why he would be given a choice is because the agents knew that he was more valuable to them on the streets then he would be locked up.

It was four p.m. on a Sunday April afternoon. Thompson and Ledgeworth sat in a white unmarked Ford Taurus on a long side street off of Lexington Avenue. Their informant had unknowingly led them to this area unaware of the fact he was being trailed. Benny Thompson held a pair of powerful binoculars to his eyes. He could see clearly into the green Jaguar that was parked up the street. Its driver appeared to be waiting for someone. Moments later a black Mustang GT with heavily tinted windows pulled behind the Jag' and parked.

Soon Kay Cee stepped out and walked to the passenger's side of the Mustang. Agent Ledgeworth snapped numerous pictures of Kay Cee getting into the black car. The driver of the GT was hidden behind the extremely dark windows. Ledgeworth adjusted the lens and zoomed in close enough to snap a few pictures of the license plate.

"What's up Papi? How is everything?" Kay Cee asked as he sat in the passenger seat and slammed the door shut.

"Everything is good," the young Dominican man said with a smile. He then reached around and began fondling with a baby's car seat in the back. He pulled out a package that was tightly wrapped in plastic. When he handed it over Kay Cee said, "Papi, I asked for two!"

"Sorry my friend I only brought one," the Spanish man replied apologetically.

Kay Cee reached into a brown paper bag and pulled out three stacks of hundred dollar bills held in a knot by rubber bands. He handed the money over to Papi, and then refolded the paper bag. Kay Cee stuffed the powdery white package of cocaine between his belt and stomach, and then gave Papi a handshake, and said, "I'll get the other one later. You did the same shit to me last week. You no like my money? Is my money good?" Kay Cee said with a smile as he tried to sound Spanish.

"I do- your money is very good. I will make it up to you. You pay twenty-two for one next time," the Dominican drug dealer said.

"You are my man Papi. That's why I do business with you," Kay Cee said after realizing that he just received a six thousand dollar discount.

The FBI took more pictures of the Mustang pulling away, and snapped many photos of their favorite informant getting back into his luxury Jaguar with its big shiny rims.

CHAPTER EIGHT
MAJOR NIGGAH

"There's a status in life regardless of the occupation in which a man must strive to obtain. He must start from the bottom, learn from the mistakes of others, and then slowly rise to the top. There will come a time when he will have to let his presence be known in order for him to be respected. Once this happens he will very soon be able to sit amongst the elite…"

Rev. Raymond Fuller was designated by the County Jail to be the bearer of all bad news. He called inmate Tymer Miller to his office early this morning to inform him of the brutal murder of his mother. He carefully explained to him that the police found her dead in the living room of her apartment. Her death had been ruled at the moment drug related because of all the drug paraphernalia found at the scene. He further notified Kilo that there were no suspects in her death, and the police are still investigating. The reverend said that Anne's funeral would be held on April 9th at his uncle's church.

After hearing the terrible news Kilo wanted to cry. He tried to cry. He knew that crying was the natural thing for a son to do when their mother was harmed. He thought of all the things that may cause him to shed a few tears in front of the reverend on his mom's behalf, but it didn't happen.

Kilo thought of her beautiful eyes, the fact that she brought him into the world, and the fact that he'll never see her alive again. But still no tears fell. Only the memories of his sister Kimberly's bloody body came to his mind. He envisioned the many nights they were left home alone with nothing to eat and all of the times they fell asleep holding their hungry tummies. He could vividly see all of the men who used to run in and out of their house patting him on his head, and none of them stopping to say, "I'm your father!"

Kilo accepted the reverend's offer for a free phone call, and then he told him what number's to dial.

"Hello," Lisa answered.

"Hi Auntie, this is Tymer," Kilo said in a low voice.

"Hello Tymer! We were just talking about you baby. How are you doing?" she asked.

"I'm doing fine. I just found out about my mother. I guessed she's gone now, huh?"

"Yes baby, it sure was a tragedy. But you need to be strong honey. No matter how bad it may seem you have to believe that God is working on your situation and only good will come your way," Lisa encouraged.

"It may seem bad now but believe me God won't let anything happen to you that He knows you can't handle. He's a loving God. At this time in your life I must admit that you are being put to the test. Just remember calamity and tribulations build a strong character in a person. Never question the works of God no matter how rough it gets, and you'll be alright. I promise," Lisa said.

"I know Auntie. Talking to you has made me feel so much better, and I really appreciate it," Kilo said respectfully.

"You're welcome honey. Be strong and take care of yourself in there. Here goes your uncle okay… Bye-bye."

Lisa passed the phone over to Freddie who was sitting next to her on the living room sofa. He was reading the Bible preparing for Anne's funeral sermon when Kilo first called.

"What's up nephew?" Freddie said.

"Pretty cool Uncle Freddie. How's everything going with you?" Kilo asked.

"It's all going okay for me so far. I try my best to keep things in order, but there are some stuff I just can't control. Your mother Oleanne is in a better place right now son. Her soul is at peace and she is no longer running the streets."

"I know, but I just never imagined her dying before. I was always hoping for the day when she would clean herself up and grow into a respectable woman," Kilo said with disappointment in his voice.

"It just happens like this sometimes. It's out of our control. Life must go on... Before I forget Tymer, when does your trial start again?"

"In two weeks on April 20th. I hope to see you and Aunt Lisa there too," Kilo responded.

"Surely we will definitely be there Tymer! Lisa and I, along with the whole church congregation will be in attendance. We pray for you in church every Sunday. You have so many faithful and loving folks on your side that all against you will fail. Just believe in your innocence and be strong," Freddie encouraged.

"Okay, I will. My time is up on the phone so I guess I'll see you next week at my mother's funeral," Kilo said.

"So they are letting you come, huh?" Freddie asked.

"These white people know that I will act a fool if they don't."

"Okay I'll see you then... You know I still got that put up for you safely. It'll be waiting for you when you are released!" Freddie said with a smile knowing that his nephew knew exactly what he was referring to.

It was broad daylight in Marketview Heights. With a small crowd of spectators watching as Smooth C held a huge .40 Cal to the side of the kids head. Everybody silently prayed he wouldn't pull the trigger.

"Niggah if I ever catch you on my block selling that bullshit wax again I'll blow your fucking head off!" Smooth C said coldly. "Matter of fact, strip you bitch ass niggah!"

Smooth C had caught the imitation drug dealer selling 'dummy bags' of crack on the Strip. He had recently claimed this particular corner as his own because of the new drug spot he just opened a few houses down. When he caught the young kid selling fake bags up there it gave him the perfect opportunity to show how serious he was about getting money.

Bystanders watched intently as the young man frantically removed his clothing just as Smooth C had ordered. Hustlers from Marketview Heights crowded around in laughter while concerned residents stood in their doorways hoping Cedric wouldn't pull the trigger.

"Nah Motherfuckah take your boxers off too!" Smooth C said while pointing his gun at the kid's ass. He wanted to pop him but it was too many onlookers. The last thing he wanted to happen was word getting back to his mother, and then having to hear one of her endless sermons. Plus he didn't want to really jeopardize losing the stake he currently had in the hood.

Smooth C was no longer driving his old red Honda Accord. That was in his mother's garage while he cruised around the city in his new cream Lexus with TV's in the headrests. He was now buying a half of kilogram of cocaine from Kay Cee twice a week. To be only eighteen years old Smooth C was doing his thing. He literally blew up overnight.

After the young kid took off his boxers Smooth C told him, "Start running pussy and I better not catch you up here again!"

With no hesitation the kid ran straight towards the bridge leading to Downtown while holding his private parts. Everybody in the crowd was dying in laughter until Smooth C turned around and said, "The next niggah to violate me, my block, or anybody I fuck with are going to feel some of these hot bullets. I'm done playing with you lame niggahs up here. Nobody sell shit on this corner unless your coke came from me."

Smooth C scanned the crowd for faces that resembled disbe-
lievers, but no one challenged him. They all knew that he was af-
filiated with Kilo and Kay Cee. Ordinary people in the hood was
looking at him as if he had lost his damn mind, but the hustlers
knew exactly what was going on with him. He was just another
young niggah trying to come up in Marketview Heights.

Smooth C stuck the gun back on his waist, and then jumped
into his Lexus that was parked at the curb. Before he sped off he lit
a blunt from the ashtray. He wished that Kilo was home. There was
a rumor going around that Kay Cee was snitching. He didn't know
how to tell Kilo about the situation without starting some serious
beef between them. It was two things Smooth C did know; he had
to stop buying his cocaine from Kay Cee, and secondly he had to
tell Kilo about the rumors sooner or later.

After a ten minute drive Smooth C parked in front of a large
housing complex on the cities Southside. A girl he just met named
Candice told him to come to apartment 5A at four o'clock. He was
sitting in the parking lot smoking the rest of his blunt when his cell
phone rung. "What up?" he answered.

"Boy what in the fuck is your problem? You didn't learn shit
from Kilo…" Kiki screamed at him without a greeting. Her home girl
Regina called and told her that Cedric made a boy that was about
sixteen years old strip and run over the bridge butt ass naked. She
told Kiki that somebody needed to talk to Smooth C because she
never saw him act this way.

"What in the hell are you talking about?" Smooth C said in an
attempt to play stupid.

"You know what I'm talking about niggah! Don't play crazy… Do
not call me when your ass ends up in jail. You already know that
you will not have any friends to depend on. All them fake ass dudes
want to do is take your place and fuck your bitches," Kiki warned.

"Yea your right Sis', but how am I supposed to keep you rocking Prada and Gucci, pay Mommy's rent, and ball until I fall if I let

niggahs disrespect my block?" he asked.

"Do you really think I give a damn about all that materialistic shit? I can buy my own stuff Cedric. What really matters is that my brother is safe. Kilo thought the same thing, and look where he's at now. Money don't mean nothing if you can't enjoy it."

"Keisha you're absolutely right. I'm going to chill from now on. I'm glad you called me baby. Sometimes a niggah need to get checked from time to time. Even if it's by his punk ass sister," Smooth C said laughing.

"Whatever. If you don't slow down I'll show you who the punk is alright... Cedric you know Kilo's trial starts the day after tomorrow, right? He'll be pissed if you don't show up. He told me to tell you that too," Kiki informed.

"I'm glad you told me because I forgot. I thought it was next week. I'll be there. I know my man is going to beat that case... Keisha I'm going to come by your house and chill with you later. I'm at one of my bitch's house right now and you're holding me up. I love you. Bye."

"Okay. I love you too!"

Smooth C hung up with his concerned sister, got out of the car and headed towards Candice's apartment. He ignored the niggahs standing in front of the building that was looking at him like a foreigner as he walked by. He thought, '*I wish one of these niggahs would act stupid.*'

Smooth C walked up to apartment 5A, and then knocked lightly on the door. After a moment Candice opened the door with a big smile once she saw who her visitor was. She was light-skinned with pretty brown eyes. Her hair was long enough to easily fall onto her shoulders. You could tell that she was a thick woman even though the hunter green bathrobe she wore covered her body.

"Smooth C I'm glad you came by. I need to run upstairs for a minute, but you could wait for me in the living room," she said while giving him a tight hug before jogging up the stairway.

When Smooth C walked into the living room he was surprised

to notice her friend sitting on the couch watching *Belly*. She was the same female who was with Candice when they met at the mall last week. She was gorgeous in her own way. This was the girl he really wanted to talk to, but Candice had been very aggressive. He wasn't really attracted to all of the body piercings Candice had. She had a ring in her eyebrow, a tongue ring, and a belly button ring. He wasn't too mad because from past experiences he knew that all those piercings meant she was a cold blooded f-r-e-a-k.

"What's going on home girl? My name is Smooth C, but you can just call me −Cee," he said extending his hand in her direction.

"I know who you are boy. I'm Dana. I've been hearing a lot about you lately. Candice hasn't stopped talking about your ass since we saw you in the mall," she said while wetting her lips with her juicy tongue.

Dana had on a pair of tight blue Apple Bottom jeans. Smooth C saw what he'd been attracted to before. She was thick as hell. He could clearly see her round nipples poking through the yellow tank top shirt she wore. At nineteen, Candice and Dana both could be models. They possessed the look and bodies for it.

When Candice walked into the room he was upset that she went and sat on the couch with Dana. "Damn girl you could have come over here to sit with me. I don't bite."

"I figured that about you, but she does," Candice said returning his smile.

Dana turned off the flat screen TV and cut on the CD player with the same remote. The soulful voice of Mary J. Blige filled the room. Candice seductively unfastened the belt to shed her robe. Smooth C couldn't believe his eyes when he saw her naked body underneath. Candice stared over at him as she slowly ran her finger across her stomach and into her wet womanhood. She circled her finger around the inside, then pulled it out and slowly slid it into Dana's mouth.

Smooth C pulled the blunt from behind his ear, and asked, "Can I smoke in here?"

Both girls replied, "Yea."

Smooth C lit the blunt, took a deep pull, and then he slid back into the butter soft leather couch to enjoy the show. Dana stood up and slowly pulled her tank top over her head. She instantly revealed her big round nipples. She gently squeezed both of them before she dropped on her knees and crawled between Candice's legs. She spread Candice's pussy lips apart with her forefingers, and then she began licking her wet sex spot.

Smooth C watched from across the room. He admired the tattoo of roses on the small of Dana's back. The sight of her round ass bent over before him and the sounds of the two women combined to cause him to become aroused. He grabbed a hold of his dick through his sweatpants, and then kicked off his black Air Force ones. He was more than ready to join in on the loving that was going down between the ladies.

Candice was moaning loudly while caressing her breast together when Smooth C walked over and sat in Dana's old seat. He rubbed Candice's full breasts while she began massaging his manhood. Candice pulled his dick out of his sweatpants, and then slowly stroked it up and down while Dana stood up to pull off her jeans. Candice bent down and started sucking on Smooth C carefully. Her mouth was warm and inviting.

Dana walked over to her purse and retrieved a row of condoms. She had a body like Ki Toy. Her ass was extremely round. When she came back over she competed with Candice at sucking on Smooth C's hard-on. They both did their best to make him feel like a king. When he exploded they fought for every drop he released.

"Hold on. Let me take off these sweatpants so we could start fucking," Smooth C said as he stood up.

"I know that's right!" Candice said while plunging two fingers inside of her wetness.

Dana fell back onto the middle of the floor. Her legs was spread wide open, and the wetness surrounded her pussy. Candice left the couch to join Dana on the soft white carpet. She returned the favor by sucking on Dana's throbbing clitoris.

Smooth C slammed his gun into his pants pocket, and then quickly stripped off all his clothes. He got down on his knees and put himself into Dana's mouth. She sucked on him until it became hard again, then he rolled on a condom before entering Candice from behind while she remained buried in Dana's womanly love.

While he was stroking Candice he looked at the passionate faces of the two ladies and thought of how much he loved black women. Some of them were freaks, but they were still beautiful creations. He thought about Kilo's trial. He wanted nothing more than for Kilo to come home so he could prove to him that he was serious about getting money now.

Thinking so much during the sex caused Smooth C to fuck Candice and Dana for hours. The three enjoyed many different sexual positions before they fell asleep.

Smooth C woke up to realize that he was still on the floor, and Candice was resting her head on his stomach with his dick inches away from her mouth. Dana had climbed up onto the couch and was sleeping with her legs spread open. He looked around and quickly remembered the fulfilling sex they all shared. He smiled while looking at Dana's hairy bush, and as he began to grow again he pushed himself back towards Candice's mouth. '*Damn it feels good to be a major niggah,*' he thought.

CHAPTER NINE

JUDGMENT DAY

"The guilty must suffer the consequences for their wrong deeds. Likewise, the innocent shall be set free. If you live by a sword, you shall die by it. If you live by the bullet, one shall pierce your flesh. If you lie, you will be lied to. We all know the so-called maxims that are supposed to be universally recognized as true. But some people can live by the sword, and avoid dying from being stabbed with one. Many lie and receive honesty. But no man commits a bad deed and escapes from his judgment day..."

The Supreme courtroom was packed with family, friends, and enemies. Deputies filled the entire back wall and about ten more officers stood post outside of the door. This had been the atmosphere during the whole week long trial. Raheem's family was seated on the left side of the courtroom. Kilo's relatives and supporters sat to the right. Yesterday Kiki and Raheem's cousin Tasha got into a heated argument after leaving court. Both women had to be escorted out of the building by dozens of deputies. Today they were allowed to return. Raheem's mother Terry had been crying all week. The deceased man's son was in the front row sitting on his mother's lap. He looked to be about four years old, and too young to understand what was taking place. Kay Cee, Kiki, and Freddie sat in the front also, but they were on the right side. Lisa, Smooth C, Renee, Regina, and a few brothers and sisters from Freddie's church sat in the last row. Everybody was gathered today to witness firsthand the fate of one man. The hearts of the courtroom was filled with many mixed emotions. Many wished for the worse, and some prayed for the best outcome possible for Tymer Miller.

Judge Dandrinch was presiding over the murder case. He was an old frail looking white man who wore a pair of small glasses that fell to the tip of his nose. The judge had a good reputation for giving black defendants a fair trial, but the ones who were found guilty often received harsh sentences for the smallest offenses. He once sentenced a man to fifteen years for driving drunk and crashing into an unoccupied police cruiser. Any defendant who was convicted of murder was more than likely to spend at least twenty-five years to life in prison if Judge Dandrinch was their sentencing judge.

The prosecutor in the case was a small white lady with a short haircut. She argued during trial that it was Tymer Miller who fired three shots from a .22 caliber pistol at Raheem McCullough. Which only one projectile managed to hit him just under his left eye before continuing into his brain. She explained to the jury that the whole incident started when Raheem failed to pay a twenty dollar debt to Mr. Miller whose street name is Kilo, after a lost round in a dice game. After a brief argument over the money Mr. Miller then pulled out an automatic handgun, and then murdered McCullough in a total disregard for human life. She also noted to the jury that even though her case was now mainly speculation- there was a young woman who witnessed the cold blooded murder while walking her child in the park that day. And before her untimely demise she stood more than willing to testify as to what she saw. The young gentle looking prosecutor in her most sincere voice begged the jury not to let the defendant escape his punishment for murder. "His street name is Kilo because he sold lots of drugs in his neighborhood. He's the reason that law abiding citizens are held hostage in their homes. The day he pulled that trigger Tymer Miller's callous actions stole a life from a child, a mother, and a fiancée," she ended.

Kilo and his lawyer Brian Mashaw sat behind a large wooden table. Brian Mashaw was recognized in Rochester as one of the best defense attorney's in the city. From day one he told Kilo that the charges against him wouldn't stick. He easily picked the case apart during the trial calling the prosecutions witness' substitutes for Danasha Graham. He went on to note that there was never a weapon found with his client's fingerprints. There was no sufficient testimony to validate with the deceased woman's statements. He argued that his client couldn't have been the shooter because he was at home with his girlfriend of ten years at the time of the homicide. "I sincerely express the deepest remorse for the victims involved in this case. It has been a long week and I want to thank the jury for being so patient, and listening to the evidence. Ladies and gentlemen justice is not only about finding and punishing the guilty. It is also most importantly finding and setting free the innocent. Today we have found an innocent man, and his name is Tymer Miller," Brian Mashaw said as he pointed over to Kilo, then asking the jury to return with a verdict of not guilty of murder in the second degree.

Before the trial started last week Kilo cut off his braids and got a brush cut in order to look nice in front of the jury. He casually sported a dark blue pin-striped Armani suit with a pair of clear frames covering his eyes. He looked like an intelligent college student, but that was just on the top layer. Deep down inside he knew that he would always be Kilo from Marketview Heights no matter which verdict the jury came back with.

The courtroom became completely quiet when Judge Dandrinch announced, "Can I have the courts attention please? The jury has notified the court that they have reached a verdict in the case of people versus Tymer Miller. Could you please escort the jury back into court?"

Kilo became extremely nervous as his hands started to shake. He closed his eyes, and said a silent prayer. "Father my time is in your hands. Please let me walk from this courtroom as an innocent man."

Kiki blew a kiss to Kilo, and then crossed her fingers. "Please God. Please," she said.

Freddie wrapped his arm around Kiki's shoulders, and then bowed his head for a moment of prayer also.

One at a time the twelve jurors walked back into the courtroom taking their respective seats. There were only three black faces. Two of them were women. None of them made eye contact with Kilo the whole time they were sitting down. That made him even more uncomfortable. He was looking for some type of assurance that everything would be okay for him.

"Juror number one please stand before the court," the clerk asked.

Juror number one was designated as the head juror. She was a spiteful looking old woman. She had a head full of grey hair that only enhanced the paleness of her skin. Her face was as red as blood, and she appeared to be extremely racist.

"Have you as a jury reached a conclusive verdict in this case?" the court's clerk asked.

"Yes we have," the head juror announced.

"Okay. In the case of people versus Tymer Miller, for the crime of murder in the second degree, how do you find the defendant?"

After a long pause, the old racist looking white woman said, "NOT GUILTY!"

The courtroom exploded with mixed emotions. There could be heard shouts of joy, and some cries of pain. Kilo was later ordered to be released from custody immediately…

———※《●》※———

Kiki waited patiently outside of the building where Kilo was to be released. She'd been waiting since 2 pm by herself. Everyone else claimed to have had something important to do, but left her with messages to give Kilo when he came out. Thanks to a speedy trial only four months had passed her by and that was long enough; she wanted to wait on her man. She couldn't believe that he had actually been acquitted and was about to be freed. Kiki anxiously watched the doors of the Public Safety Building from her brand new black Mercedes Benz. When she finally saw Kilo emerge from the building her heart momentarily stopped in time.

Kilo stood in front of the building and quickly inhaled the fresh air deep inside of his lungs. He noticed that the sky seemed bluer and the budding trees were even greener than last summer. His eyes had become too accustomed to seeing the monotony of beige walls throughout the entire jail. It was like he had been given his sight back after being blinded for four months.

Kilo looked around before he spotted his baby girl Kiki running across the street in his direction. He could see her bright white teeth from where he stood. She was the most beautiful woman he ever knew. When she finally reached him he immediately wrapped her up into a tight and warm hug. Neither one said a word. Kiki began to passionately kiss him on his neck as he picked her up and spun her around.

"I missed you Kilo," she said breaking the silence. A small tear was rolling down her cheek.

"I missed you too baby. Where are you parked at? I want to get as far away from this place as possible…Yes!" Kilo shouted. The way he felt inside was unexplainable. It was almost like dying, and then coming back to life with a chance to correct past mistakes.

"Damn Kiki," Kilo said as he approached his girl's new Benz. "You didn't tell me you hooked your car up like this baby. Five star rims. TV's all in the headrests. Four months ago you were driving a broke down Honda. I really like this car though."

"Boy you know damn well that I'm not into the flashy shit. I let Cedric hold it last week and this is how he brought it back. Pimped… I was about to curse his ass out until he showed me this iced out Michael Kors watch he gave me," she explained.

"That watch is hot too, but why are you cursing so much?" Kilo asked seriously.

Kiki smiled, and said, "I'm sorry. I'm just so happy your home right now that I'm getting a little besides myself. Thank you Jesus!" She knew that Kilo couldn't stand for a female to curse or smoke cigarettes. He believed that the two were unladylike, and it also reminded him of a "hood rat". The only thing that he expected from Kiki was that she carried herself with class at all times.

Kilo quickly jumped into the driver's seat while Kiki played the passenger.

"Baby, Kay Cee told me to give you this stuff. Everybody acted like they couldn't wait for you to get out… Your uncle said call as soon as you get a chance, or just stop by his house," Kiki said. She then opened up the glove compartment in front of her, and then pulled out a huge platinum, diamond chain with an expensive iced-out Virgin Mary emblem on it. Then she reached back inside and pulled out a stack of hundred dollar bills. "Kay Cee said it was three grand, but I didn't count it."

Kilo couldn't stop smiling.

"Last but not least, I know you want this," Kiki said. She grabbed two fifty dollar bags of light green weed and a box of Phillies blunts from the glove compartment.

"Oh shit! My son Kay Cee looked out for a niggah. I love this chain," he said while letting the diamond necklace hang over his crispy white tee.

Kilo rolled up a blunt. After he put fire to its end, he was ready to roll out. He jumped on the expressway and drove straight to the mall. While they were riding Kiki told him that Kay Cee was throwing him a party tonight at the Hyatt Hotel. Kay Cee had made the early arraignments because he knew Kilo was coming home. He had alleviated most of the risk of him being convicted by murdering Danasha.

At the mall Kilo spent the whole three grand. He bought a few pairs of sneakers and Timberlands, and about five outfits. After leaving the mall he drove out to his house in Webster, New York. It was a nice and quiet suburb of Rochester. He felt good when he finally pulled into the driveway alongside his beautiful home.

Kiki had the house spotless. Kilo walked around inspecting it to see if there was any evidence of Kiki not being a good girl while he was gone, but everything still looked damn near the same.

"Boy you better take your shoes off on my white carpet. The man just came to clean it two days ago," Kiki said as she ran up the stairs with her shopping bags.

"Kiki, this is still my house! Don't get it fucked up because it's in your name, and I've been gone for a while... I run shit!" he yelled behind her playfully.

"Whatever!" she yelled back.

Kilo went into the kitchen and warmed up some macaroni & cheese he found in the refrigerator. He made himself comfortable in the living room and started watching B.E.T on the 52" plasma TV that Kiki must have just purchased recently. It felt great to finally be back in the privacy of his home again. He thought back to the 'House of Pain' and the many young brothers who weren't as fortunate as him. Like the ones who really had to experience the prison life. Many of them had been sentenced to life behind bars. One kid named, Killa from the Westside was only nineteen years old and sentenced to natural life for shooting a cop and killing an innocent bystander. One day Kilo asked young Killa, "How do young players like you get caught up in this game so seriously? Niggahs be having so much fucking potential." Killa responded, "I blame the older niggahs who make this shit look like the streets is the only way."

For once in Kilo's life he could truly relate to the other side of the struggle. Jail was no place for a man to be and it definitely wasn't anywhere he wanted to go again. His new wealth of understanding made him appreciate the fact that his couch was soft as hell. He respected that the room temperature was just right, and that his girl had the house smelling wonderful.

Kilo was relaxing on the coach watching 106 & Park when Kiki yelled from the top of the stairs, "Kilo baby come here for a minute!" Kilo got up and went into the kitchen to put his empty plate in the sink, and then he headed up the stairs. "I'm in the bathroom honey."

Kilo walked to the door of the bathroom and stood there as he watched his beautiful woman sitting in the huge tub with her hair hanging down. The bathroom smelled like fresh strawberries. The bubbles in the tub hid Kiki's nakedness. Kilo stood there admiring her beauty, eyes, smile, and pecan complexion.

"Are you going to stand there all day, or are you going to join your lady?" she asked in a welcoming manner.

"I have no problem watching you all day."

"Too bad because I need for you to do more than watch."

Kiki looked on as Kilo began to remove his clothes. She noticed that he had toned up since being in jail. He even had a six pack and muscles now. Kilo slowly stepped into the warm water. He sat facing Kiki, and said, "I thought about you every day in there. I love you Keisha."

"Keisha huh, I love you too Tymer."

They both shared a smile before kissing each other deeply. Kiki slid her hand beneath the bubbles grabbing a hold of his manhood. He began to palm her ass with both hands while she stroked him. He tried to lift her on top of him, but she stopped his efforts.

"Hold up Kilo," she said before he could enter her. "I want to do something for you. I was going to do it the night you went to jail… stand up."

Kilo looked at her funny, and then stood up in the tub like she asked. His erection stretched out in her direction. Kiki slowly rose to her knees. She wiped the bubbles from his stomach and his manhood. She slowly slid him into her mouth while staring deep into his eyes. "Ah," was the only word he could muster. She took her time and licked her man's dick with love. He couldn't believe she was sucking and licking all over his erection.

Kilo stopped her before he could reach his climax. He picked her up into his arms and carried her wet body into their bedroom.

He softly laid her back on the middle of the huge bed. Returning the favor Kilo sucked on her. He gently pulled her lower lips apart and licked both sides while he flicked his tongue over them. She began screaming and moaning as she clutched the sheets with her hands during her first orgasm.

"Kilo baby make me feel good!" she cooed.

Kilo got on top of her body, and then passionately slid himself deep inside of her warm pussy. Kiki tightly wrapped around him with the grip of a virgin.

Her sweet womanly juices began to flow all over as he slid in and out. It flowed on the sheets, down her legs, and all over Kilo's face as he went back below. They made love to each other with a lasting passion they both will never forget.

CHAPTER TEN
SCAR OF WISDOM

"**E**xperience is the best teacher in the game of life. So often it takes a tragedy for a person to decide to change their ways. It's unfortunate because that realization of wrong was always within. The longer a person lives, the more he learns. It is he who lives and learns from experience and eventually gains the most wisdom. If you listen to his story, he may be able to save you from the often fatal grasp of a tragedy happening to you..."

Cars overcrowded the small hotel parking lot across from the Hyatt Hotel in downtown Rochester. Some automobiles were double parked along the streets. On the ramp there was no place to park anymore. There was a long line of people pushing and arguing with each other wanting to be next to get into the party. Kay Cee had passed out flyers and even had the event announced on WDKX, a local radio station. After hearing the advertisement on the radio the whole town rushed to the mall to make sure they had something new to wear tonight. Anytime someone from Marketview Heights through a party it was sure to be live.

When Kilo slowly rolled past the hotel in Kiki's Benz he could see into the lobby through the front glass and it looked like it was packed. Kiki decided to stay home and get some sleep. She made

Kilo promise that he'd come back home and wouldn't stay out all night.

Kilo was wearing a black Atlanta Falcons fitted cap and a plain black tee shirt that enhanced the shining power of his jewelry. His jeans were made by Request and he sported a pair of black suede construction Timberlands. He found the closest available parking space, which was a little ways from the hotel. Just in case, he stuffed a small .22 caliber revolver down the inside of his boot. He knew that old beef didn't die and it was better to get caught with a gun than without one. All eyes were on Kilo as he walked past the long line leading up to the entrance. There were groups of beautiful females everywhere and they were dressed in their best outfits. The attention Kilo was receiving from the ladies made him feel like a million bucks.

"Kilo...Kilo!" a pretty brown-skinned female called from the line as he passed.

"What's up Dominique?" Kilo said recognizing her from the hood.

"Let us get in with you, please. We've been waiting in this line for hours," she begged.

"Who are you with?"

"Just us," she said while pointing back to about ten more ladies.

"Damn you deep as hell. But come on. You from the hood so fuck it," Kilo said.

They wasted no time as they all hurried out of the line. Other females whispered hatred and jealously twisted up their faces into frowns.

Kay Cee stood at the front door with three big black bouncers. They looked to be ready and willing to put hands on anyone who decided to act stupid tonight. Kay Cee was wearing a Roc-A-Wear jean suit. His diamonds were glistering. His face lit up in excitement when he noticed Kilo coming, and being followed by about ten dime pieces.

"There goes my niggah!" Kay Cee shouted.

The two slapped fives and embraced in a brotherly hug. "What's up Kay Cee?" Kilo said.

"Shit niggah you the man. I see you still love the ladies. Who are these sexy young things you got?" Kay Cee asked while scanning the crowd of beautiful women behind Kilo.

"That's Dominique and her peoples. They from Marketview Heights," Kilo said as he motioned for them to go inside. "Fam' you don't know how good it feels to be out of that fucking place."

"I can almost imagine Kilo."

"Kay Cee man I really, from the heart, appreciate how you laid your gangsta' down for me. You the realist motherfuckah I know... and the sharpest too. You're going to make me tuck my shit in with that big ass chain you rocking!"

"Stop it Kilo..." Kay Cee said blushing. "But on that other note, I would do it again if the situation ever presented itself. You my niggah and that shit means more to me than anything. But that is the past now so start enjoying yourself... Welcome home!"

After an hour passed Kilo was already dead ass drunk. He had tossed back about five shots of Remy Martin and three cups of Gin & Juice. Now he was working on a bottle of Crown Royal. Kilo played the wall as he watched the dancing crowd. Kay Cee ran around making sure things were in order. Everybody and their momma's seemed to be at the party. Every time Kilo turned around someone different was approaching him to wish him well. Smooth C was there too for a little while. He just left with a sexy ass Spanish mommy. Before he staggered out of the door he told Kilo, "I'll see you tomorrow niggah. I'm about to go fuck the shit out of this bitch."

The hotel's ballroom was gigantic. Kilo couldn't count how many beautiful women were there. Everywhere he looked it was a crowd of fine ladies dancing and enjoying themselves. He was glad that Kiki chose to stay home because he had his eyes set on a few potential freaks.

The Dee Jay stopped the music, and shouted through the microphone, "What's happening Rochester, New York! I need for you to give it up for my man Kilo... He's one of Marketview Heights finest and most respected. Welcome home my niggah!" The crowd excitedly sung along when the Dee Jay played, 'Welcome Back' by Mase.

Kilo loved the attention he was getting. He was definitely back. "Excuse me sexy, could you hold this bottle for me real quick?" he whispered into the female standing next to him ear. He needed to free his hands while he twisted up another blunt.

The beautiful woman took the bottle from Kilo and was wondering why he didn't remember her. She waited for Kilo to finish rolling his blunt and put fire to its end, and said, "Kilo you don't remember me?" he bent closer to hear her better over the loud music. "Boy this is Ebony from East High School!"

Kilo stepped back and looked her up and down. Ebony was brown-skinned with long hair that was tied back into a pony tail. Her tan shorts highlighted her thick thighs. She had on I long gold chain that hung down between her well-shaped breasts. He hadn't noticed her because of the Burberry hat she wore covering her head down to her sexy eyes.

"Yea, what's up Ebony? I haven't seen you in a while. What brings you out tonight?" Kilo whispered in her ear.

"I came to see you matter of fact. I saw a flyer that said this was your welcome home party. The least I could do was come and say hello. You know I still have feelings for you," she explained.

"Word, so is your man here? I don't want to have to knock out no jealous ass niggah... I'm already fresh out of jail!" Kilo said laughing.

"Nah I'm by myself."

"So do you plan on leaving that way or with me?" Kilo asked.

"Hopefully I can go with you tonight," she replied with a smile.

Kilo and Ebony had a little history together dating back when they were in high school. Five years ago was the last time they had spoken to one another and since then Kilo could see that she had definitely grown up. There was just no way he planned on passing up this ass tonight.

"Well it's not any need waiting around in here. I already had my little fun," Kilo said before taking a puff from his blunt.

Ebony grabbed a hold of his hand and led him through the dancing crowd. It was only one o'clock in the morning and Kilo figured that he had at least three more hours to kill before he had to be home in order to not raise any suspicion with Kiki.

They left the party and drove to the nearest hotel around the corner in Ebony's Hummer. Once inside the small single bed room Ebony began to tell Kilo about her life since he departed from it. She told him that she was now a model and bank teller for Bank of America. She explained that she really wanted to come visit him while he was in jail but she was afraid of being rejected. Lastly, Ebony described how happy she was to hear that he was acquitted. "I almost cried. I didn't want you to be subjected to so much pain baby."

"Girl I would have loved to see you while I was locked up. In jail sometimes a niggah be feeling dead. Somebody has to bring a brother some flowers," Kilo said while rubbing her back as he sat next to her on the edge of the bed.

Kilo explained that he was still with the same girl she knew from East and they were happy together. But at the same time he didn't want that situation to interfere with tonight and the connection they shared.

"No I understand Kilo. I remember Keisha. She was in my science class. I just want tonight to be special for us in remembrance of the good old days. She never stopped us from fucking before did she?" Ebony asked as she got up to dim the lights.

Kilo watched from the bed as she stood in the middle of the floor removing all of her clothes. This had turned out to be the best day of his life. On April 20th he thought he would be convicted of murder and later sentenced to forever in prison, and now he was in a hotel getting ready to have sex with one of his old bitches.

Ebony walked up to Kilo and stood between his legs naked. Her nipples were erect and her black skin was silky soft. He used his hands to explore the many curves of her lovely frame. He sucked on her pointy nipples as he caressed her soft ass cheeks. She stood before him loving his every touch. Kilo slowly slid his index finger along her wet split before plunging it into her opening.

Ebony gently pushed him back on the bed, and began to unzip his jeans. She pulled out his dick and slowly placed her full lips around the head. Kilo lifted up to take off his shirt while she wildly sucked on him. She stopped for a moment to allow him to remove his pants. He pulled out a condom and quickly pulled it over his hardness. Ebony climbed on top of his shaft and slid down until he filled her insides with pleasure.

Even as a teenager Kilo loved having sex with her. She knew how to move and she made the prettiest faces when his dick started hurting her. Kilo turned Ebony onto her stomach and penetrated from the back. He had to stuff two fingers inside of her mouth to muffle her loud screams as he pounded her pussy with no remorse. The love making ended in the shower with him releasing into her welcoming mouth for the second time of the night.

<hr />

Kilo slowly pulled up in front of a small white house with burgundy trimmings. His uncle Freddie lived in the 19th ward of Rochester. This part of the Westside was nice, but there were other neighborhoods a few blocks away that were murder central. Like for instance Genesee and Sawyer, or Plymouth and Bartlett Avenues. Kilo made it his business not to have many dealings with hustlers from the Westside. They had a bad reputation for crossing good niggahs for small amounts of money. Many of them even resorted to robbing each other when times were rough. On the other hand, Kay Cee would do business with anybody from anywhere. If your money was green he had what you needed, regardless of what side of the river you was from. Kilo often predicted that Kay Cee's greed would be his downfall in the streets.

Kilo lightly knocked on his uncle's front door three times. After a while Lisa opened the door wearing a pink sweat suit by Baby Phat. Her long black hair was tied into a pony tail, and she was all smiles, "Hi Tymer!"

"What's up Lisa," Kilo said as he received her into his arms for a hug.

"Baby I told you to have faith, didn't I? Now you need to do right by God. He gave you another chance."

"Of' course I will. I know how blessed I am auntie," Kilo said convincingly. He followed Lisa down the short corridor. He stopped for a moment to look at a picture of his mother Anne, when she first moved to Rochester hanging on the wall. She had a big smile on her young beautiful face. The photo kind of reminded him of how peaceful she looked in her casket.

When he reached the all-white living room Freddie came from out of the kitchen holding a glass of orange juice. He was a tall brown complexioned man with salt and pepper hair. "Hey there's my favorite nephew!"

"What's up Unc'?" Kilo said as he walked up to give Freddie a tight hug.

"Come upstairs with me Tymer I want to show you something… Lisa, make your nephew something to eat. We'll be right back. Come on son," Freddie said.

Freddie's huge bedroom was decorated in all white just like the living room. His house always reminded Kilo of a small palace. On every wall of the bedroom he had a portrait of a famous black person. They were mostly pictures of civil rights leaders and famous poets. Over the King-sized bed was a picture of Malcolm X. Down stairs Kilo remembered seeing a picture of Dr. Martin Luther King and W.E.B Dubois in the living room. Freddie had a book case with over a thousand different titles in the corner of the room. Kilo randomly picked one up and it was the biography of Jesse Jackson by Marshell Frady.

"Tymer that's what you need to do read some of those books about your history. One book could open up a whole new realm of understanding for you. Some of those black men and women risked and even lost their lives so you could enjoy a little freedom today," Freddie said from inside of his walk in closet.

"I know Unc' I've been doing a lot of thinking about history the last couple of months. I read a few books in jail too. I read the biography of Marcus Garvey and Sojourner Truth. I never knew that Marcus Garvey had over two million followers," Kilo reported.

"Yes he did," Freddie said as he emerged from the closet holding a long double barrow shotgun, and also two black duffle bags. "Boy you left me here with all of this money... I had to go out and buy me some protection."

Kilo started dying laughing. He had heard many stories about his uncle's hay days, but he looked too funny carrying that big ass gun. "Unc' what are you going to do with that? Man you going to mess around and kill somebody."

"Don't be fooled boy... back in my days I was something else. The devil really had my soul. Not to brag on my past sins but I've been doing this since Baghdad, since you was in your dad's bag!" Freddie said causing Kilo to erupt into more laughter.

Over the years Freddie had always kept Kilo's money, but he had gotten nervous when Kiki brought him over $80,000 dollars. Kilo didn't want the stick up kids to follow Kiki home while he was in jail and rob her, so he made her take his stash to Freddie until everything was settled.

"So what do you plan on doing with all of this money Tymer?" Freddie asked as he handed over the duffle bags.

"I'm going to take fifty thousand now and the rest you can have!"

Freddie wasn't even excited by the offer, he simply said, "Tymer you sure should leave those streets alone now. When I changed my life I only had seventeen thousand dollars to my name. I gave my bottom girl Diamond two grand and I never once looked back. That was twenty-five years ago, and nephew I submit to you that it was the best decision I ever made."

"Unc' if you don't mind me asking… what made you walk away from the pimping game?"

Freddie tossed the shotgun softly on the bed. Kilo noticed tears starting to form in the old man's eyes. "For two reasons Tymer."

He walked up to Kilo, and then slowly began to lift up the front of his tee shirt. He revealed a long ugly scar that ran from the bottom of his chest all the way down his stomach. Kilo could see small bullet holes misplaced around the scar.

"I was shot six times Tymer… six times. This was the first reason. I was on my death bed fighting for my young life. The doctors told me that if I lived I would never walk or talk again. I called on God and told him that if he made those people out to be liars… if I could walk and if I ever speak another word then I would change my life, and walk and talk in His name," Freddie said while wiping the tears from his face. "Kilo, when I walked out of that hospital shouting the Lord's name ten months later… that was reason number two."

"Wow Unc' that's deep. I never knew you had gotten shot before," Kilo said surprised.

"I never tell anybody. Not even in testimonials do I mention it. You lived with me for many years and never knew. Only your mother, Lisa, and now you have ever seen my scar. I used to hide it from women for years until I met Lisa," Freddie explained. "Tymer you have a beautiful woman who worships the ground you walk on. You're still young, and you have lots of money. You could wash your hands at any time to escape Rochester. This city is a death trap son. Few men are able to make it out of that same neighborhood you were raised in… They tried to kill me Tymer. They wanted to take my life for something I never had to worry about. Women brought it to me every hour on the hour. I won it shooting dice, and I spent it just as fast as it came… Money! Get out of the game son."

What Kilo was hearing was the raw side of his uncle and not the preacher he knew so well. It wasn't a sermon, but real life. He had just beaten a murder charge and two days later he was prepared to be back in action like nothing ever happened. Kilo knew that soon he would have to make a life or death decision before someone else made it for him. The life of a hustler shouldn't last forever...

CHAPTER ELEVEN
EVERYBODY'S
GOING TO EAT

"To be successful as a leader in any field one must always know how to make everyone happy. Slaves grow to hate the wealth of their masters. Friends will eventually begin to envy the prosperity of their best friend. This can be worked out if one learns how to satisfy the thirst of everybody around them. Never give too much, and never give too little. And of' course there will always be those who are never satisfied..."

Early one Sunday morning Kilo found himself standing on a corner in Marketview Heights. He was holding a bottle of orange juice and had a newspaper tucked underneath his arm. This was the same block that Smooth C had claimed as his own a few weeks ago. The hood looked kind of funny after being away for so long. He watched as the hustlers sold their crack in a heated competition to make the most money. Ten hustlers would run up to one car all at once displaying their products. A "crack head" would get rushed by four or five hustlers at a time. If a hustler recognized a familiar crack head coming over the bridge, without warning he would sprint for him first, and then the race would be on. Kilo himself had passed this stage of selling drugs called, block hustling. Before going to jail he was supplying most of the crack cocaine, and operating a local spot. Kilo wanted to see who was out hustling and how hard.

"Kilo what's up?" a heavy voice called from behind. He had crept up while Kilo was busy watching a car full of females ride past in a golden Navigator.

Kilo was shocked when he turned around and saw who was standing behind him with his huge arms folded across his large chest. "What's happening Steal? When did you get out?" Kilo asked looking up into Steal's mean black face.

Steal was an old school stick up kid from back in the days. Every hood has greasy niggahs like him somewhere. He did ten years Upstate for armed robbery. It was there that he acquired the name, Steal, as he ran through maximum secure prisons like Elmira, Clinton, Comstock, and Nap Nap stabbing anyone who disrespected somebody from Rochester. Back during his jail stint niggahs from New York City was under the impression that Rochester, Buffalo, and Syracuse inmates were from the country and because of that they were soft. Steal, with the help of a few more well-known O.G's put an end to that myth as they put in work 'Up north'.

Steal was the type of person you could never trust. Standing at a dangerous six feet five inches tall and weighing three hundred pounds of straight muscle, dude was a beast. The long scar down the left side of his cheek didn't help aid his innocent look. He put a real meaning to the word "goon". After he was released from Attica Correctional Facility he continued his old profession as a stick up kid. He robbed stick up kids, who had robbed other stick up kids that robbed Dominicans for bricks. But one thing that fueled Steal's fire was the fact that stick up money didn't last long.

"I came home from the County yesterday. They couldn't hit me with a parole violation so they just reinstated me... I see you back in action again. Your young ass dodged a silver bullet. The white people wanted to hang you boy. You are a lucky little niggah," Steal said.

"Yea Steal I guess twenty-five to life just wasn't my fate. They say good things come to good niggahs," Kilo replied. He noticed that Steal couldn't take his eyes off of his platinum chain.

"Fuck all of that niggah you just lucky... Kilo, you know I'm fresh out of jail and a niggah is kind of fucked up out here... I really don't want to go back to my old ways just yet, you know."

Kilo got the message Steal was sending. He was known for strong armed robberies too, but Kilo wasn't worried about that. He knew that his 9mm was on his waist.

"I feel you Steal, word. It's rough out here in these mean streets... Those lawyer fees and all that trial shit fucked me up bad. You know Brian Mashaw be trying to bankrupt niggahs..." Kilo said looking away. "But shit niggah if you wanted to take a few grand, I know this niggah in the hood who sitting on major paper on the low!"

Steal stepped closer to the music coming from Kilo's mouth and whispered, "Who you talking about?"

"Between me and you the boy Flames is buying keys of cocaine now. That little young dusty niggah came up overnight. He asked me for a brick yesterday. But being that I'm not that strong no more I pointed him in another direction," Kilo said seriously. "The real shit is that he was riding around with the money in his trunk!"

Of' course Kilo was lying about Flames asking him for a kilogram of cocaine, but after hearing that he was tricking with his mother Anne while he was in jail, this would be payback. By sending a hungry Steal his way meant real trouble. His story sounded good to Steal because Flames had just pulled out a black Land Rover for the summer, but he definitely wasn't buying thirty thousand dollars' worth of coke yet. Steal would rob him expecting to get key money or at least a large quantity of cocaine, and when Flames couldn't produce either one he'd end up in the Riverside Cemetery pushing up daisies for sure.

"For real son, he's getting money like that?" Steal asked.

"He may be getting money harder!"

"Good looking out my niggah... I'll be seeing you around," Steal said as he turned and walked away. He wasn't stupid. He knew that

Kilo still had money. It was rumored that he was a millionaire before going to jail. The streets had a weird way of calculating a niggahs worth. Steal was also aware of the fact that he had a better chance at robbing Flames who was a coward in disguise then he did at fucking with Kilo, who was a real niggah in the flesh...

After a few months passed by things were running smooth in Marketview Heights. Kilo was making more money now in the drug game than he ever did before. His product was moving so fast that he was finally able to lower prices on the entire crack he sold. He opened up about five different drug houses all around the hood. One house was used to sell strictly weight, while the others were used to sell nickels, dimes, and twenties. By having so many houses he was able to control the amount of traffic that went to each one. For the first time Kilo even tapped into the weed market. He purchased large quantities of Indo weed from some niggahs he knew from Niagara Falls, New York and was now neck and neck with the Jamaicans in that industry too.

Kilo was now worth a half of a million dollars, but nobody could tell. He preferred to switch up in rental cars as opposed to purchasing a fancy car to drive. He gave away all of his expensive platinum jewelry to the cool young niggahs in the hood. One time when he sent Lil' Tre to the store to get ten bottles of water for the two teams playing basketball at the park, Kilo took the diamond earring out of his ear and gave it to him when he came back. "Stay in school Tre and I will always look out for you," Kilo said. The next day Tre's mom Felicia tried to return the earring saying it was too much for her son. Kilo winded up having to give her a hundred dollar bill just to keep it.

Kilo let his hair grow back after getting out of jail. He gave Dominique his iced-out watch that had diamonds flooding the bezel for braiding his hair back into simple cornrows. He also let her know that she was a perfect role model for the other girls in the hood. She was a pretty female that a niggah would love to have as a wife. Kilo gave her some advice from his male point of view, "The longer you make a niggah wait for sex, the longer you'll keep him. No man wants to make a girl he sexed in one day his wife." Before leaving her house that day he joked that she better not ever charge him for a hair due again because that was a five thousand dollar watch.

Last weekend Kilo hosted a cookout in the hood at the same park Raheem was killed. Major niggahs from all over Rochester came through the Heights to chill. Free food and drinks were served to everybody; even the neighborhood crack heads got a plate. The beautiful ladies walked around wearing hardly any clothing at all as they enjoyed the hot August weather. Niggahs from the hood ran around soaking them with big ass water guns. The whole hood was having a ball until the police came through and spoiled the summer day as usual. It seemed like they hated to see black folks together having fun, especially if there wasn't any fighting going on.

The hood loved Kilo with a passion. He was making sure that everybody was able to make money. He made it possible for lame niggahs from around the way to feed their families by fronting them crack on consignment. Hustlers who never went outside of Rochester a day in their lives were now able to travel around the United States to ball. Even the stick up kids put their guns down for the moment to take advantage of the sweet drug money. Kilo made sure that the bags of crack were bigger and the quality was next to pure so that the fiends would come from miles away just to buy drugs from Marketview Heights.

Kilo continued to buy his powder cocaine from his longtime connect Omar. He was the most low key major drug dealer in the R.O.C. He didn't even have to hustle any longer, but he was one of those niggahs that was married to the game for life. Omar was a cool fat brown-skinned dude with a low haircut. He always wore a pair of shades to cover his sleepy left eye that was damaged in a car accident years ago. Omar was the first person to give Kilo a chance to actually make some real cash. He took a gamble on Kilo and fronted the young hustler a Kilogram of cocaine. Hunger, dedication, and street smarts put Kilo in a position to never have to be fronted again. Once he paid Omar back the money he owed for the original front, he blow up quick and made sure Kay Cee was with him all the way. After all the years Kilo made sure he did business with Omar out of loyalty and respect, even though the Dominicans badly wanted his business. He allowed Kay Cee to deal with them while he faithfully went with the grain. As long as everybody was getting money Kilo was happy.

Since Kilo was making so much money he decided to invest in few businesses. He sponsored Kiki's dream, a barber shop and adjacent hair salon called 'Kiki's Beauty Shop'. It was located at a huge store front on E. Main Street just over the bridge from Marketview Heights. Kiki ran the beauty salon doing hair with a couple of females she hired. Kilo managed the barber shop side. He hired barbers that were from the hood only. He wanted to make sure the money circulated in the impoverished Marketview Heights. He wanted to give niggahs with dreams some type of reality. Kilo made his young workers go to school and made sure they received a thousand dollars a week for hustling.

Kilo felt obligated to giving back to his hood. He started standing on the block early in the morning to pass out five dollar bills to the elementary and middle school kids as they passed. Kilo helped the local church organize a summer car wash to raise money for religious field trips. After a month it generated over ten grand in sales and donations. Although he was still in the streets Kilo made sure that he attended his uncle's church at least twice a month.

Kilo and Kiki was comfortably stretched out in the back of the burgundy Rolls Royce Phantom. Kilo was sure to compliment Omar on its soft white leather interior. Kilo sat back puffing slowly on a huge blunt as he watched 'Scarface' on the TV monitor on the back of the driver's headrest. He was the only person Omar allowed to smoke inside of his cars. Kiki was fast asleep next to her man. Omar was sunk into the passenger's seat watching the gangster movie with Kilo. His beautiful wife Lacey was behind the wheel easily bending the curves of the highway. She was a chocolate queen; tall, sexy, and portrayed a lot of class. The foursome was on their way back to Rochester from a weeklong vacation in Florida. Omar owned a summer condo on the shores of Daytona Beach.

Over the vacation Kiki fell in love with the sights of Florida. She didn't want to leave. Her new dream was to buy a home and move to Miami. She loved the hot weather, the pretty palm trees, and the clear blue waters of the Florida Coast. Taking this trip helped Kilo to realize that he needed to explore the exotic places of the world instead of tie himself down to Rochester.

In a guest room of Omar's condo Kilo promised Kiki that as soon as the New Year came in they would leave the R.O.C and move to the city of her choice. "Wherever you want to live baby we'll relocate there," he said.

After putting his word on his promise they made sweet love in front of the fire place for the rest of the night. Early the next morning when he rolled over to face her, she said with a smile, "I want to move to Miami!"

"Kilo man I love what you're doing in the town. Those motherfuckahs love you in the Heights. I feel the energy when I come through now. From what I hear you that niggah," Omar said from the front seat when the movie ended.

"Yea I show love to those who deserve it. I would rather be loved than feared because a scared man will kill. But whoever don't love me must be a jealous bastard because I'm too good of a niggah," Kilo responded as he blew out a cloud of smoke.

"To be honest Kilo I wasn't going to do anymore business with you after your little run in with the law. I mean, you know how I like to move- low key so nobody knows me! But you like a brother to me Kilo. I knew deep down inside my heart that you would prosper again just like you did years ago when I first gave you that work. I'm proud of you. You didn't let me down. Shit niggah you turned into a ghetto philanthropist," Omar said. Lacey smiled at Kilo through the rearview mirror.

"I figure that since I'm making a couple dollars now I should give back, you know. I hate to see people comfortable with being fucked up. Before you put me on Omar I was a lost young niggah out here. Money brightened up my life, but I can't forget about the people that niggahs like us ruin to get paid. So I try to put some of that bread back into the pot as often as I can, especially for the youths."

"You have the right idea about this life shit Kilo. I wish everybody who sold crack could think like you, even me," Omar admitted. "Your leadership skills are a characteristic that people in your circle may over time come to envy. I've seen the shit happen a million times in my thirty-nine years. I'm just telling you this for your own good… watch those niggahs who's around you! It's rarely good niggahs who fall, but it's always his company that end up dragging him down for one fucked up reason or another."

Lacey exited right after passing a sign that read: **Welcome to the City of Rochester**…

CHAPTER TWELVE
YOUR BOY NOT RIGHT

"**Always keep your ears open and listen to what people are trying to tell you. Sometimes others can see the vital warning signs we often overlook. The truth hurts, but never let your emotions supersede your intelligence…**"

"Look man. If I wear a wire that shit will get me killed. These hustlers out here are not stupid. They'll detect it right away. Niggahs got a sixth sense for that kind of shit," Kay Cee cried from the back seat.

"It's either that, or you go to fucking jail Conway. We tried to cut you a break and then you turn around and spit in our face. You didn't have to murder that poor girl you sorry cock sucker!" Agent Benny Thompson said angrily.

"I didn't have anything to do with those murders. That shit happened way the fuck in Buffalo. Why would I try some shit like that knowing I have the FEDS watching my every move?" Kay Cee pleaded.

"Sure you didn't," Mike Ledgeworth intervened. "But let's forget about the homicides in Buffalo for a moment, while we concentrate on frying these bigger fish… Tell us more about Miller and this Omar guy?" he asked.

The veteran FBI agents called Kay Cee at 7am demanding an

urgent meeting that couldn't wait. Kay Cee leaned low in the back of the green unmarked Chevy Impala. He was wearing a pair of dark shades to cover his eyes and a hood from his white sweat shirt over his head. They were parked in the back parking lot of an old abandoned McDonalds. Kay Cee hated these surprise meetings because they always ended in a ride around the city. He was lucky nobody had spotted him yet. Well at least from what he could tell they hadn't.

"I told you everything I know about them two. I never really did business with Omar. Kilo does most of the dealings with him. I buy my crack from the Dominicans," Kay Cee explained to the federal cops.

"Well you light-skinned son of a bitch you didn't tell us enough to keep your mixed ass out of prison for five hundred months under project exile laws!" Benny Thompson yelled.

"So Kenny, you said that your friend Tymer Miller's street name is Kilo, and his supplier is Omar. Is this his real name?" Mike Ledgeworth asked as he prepared to write Kay Cee's response onto a notepad.

"Yea Omar is his real name, but I never knew his last name," Kay Cee said honestly.

"Well motherfuckah you better find out!" Benny Thompson screamed again.

"And exactly how many kilograms of cocaine did you say Tymer Miller could sell in a month?" Ledgeworth asked.

"He sells about ten. His business is at an all-time high. Kilo's not the only one making a lot of money either. You have Reggie Brown from the west side and Pedro Mendez from Clinton Manor selling the entire projects heroine. I'll wear a wire for those two niggahs, but Kilo is too smart... he'll know something. I mean... anything to keep my freedom," Kay Cee said desperately.

All of this started a year and a half ago when Kay Cee was pulled over with a kilogram of powder cocaine hidden in his trunk. After the Rochester Police Department found the drugs with the help of K-9 dogs they transported him to the interrogation room of the County Jail, along with the big chrome Mac 11 machine gun that was found underneath the driver's seat.

The gun and cocaine combined made Kay Cee eligible for Project Exile, which meant strict federal prosecution. With his luck agents Benny Thompson and Mike Ledgeworth came to pay him a visit. They promised that as long as he cooperated they'd postpone all of his future court dates and when they were satisfied he would be cut loose. He'd be as free as a singing bird. At that moment when he failed to tell them both to kiss his natural black ass; he willingly and literally sold his soul to the devil. Although the price wasn't cheap, he could have had easily been serving twenty-five years or more in federal prison. Instead he was free on an ankle bracelet telling on everybody and their momma's.

"Let's take a ride Conway. We would like to see a few of these places you've told us about. Is that okay with you?" Mike Ledgeworth asked as if he had a choice.

"How could I say no? Just please don't ride through Marketview Heights again!" Kay Cee begged.

—————)((O))(——————

"Kilo, you heard about the police finding the niggah Flames in his house dead last night, right?" Smooth C asked.

Kilo immediately thought of Steal. He figured that Steal had finally tried to rob the niggah who he thought had money now. Kilo felt bad for Flames, but at the same time he knew that this was the outcome for those who crossed the line of a niggahs pride.

"Word, where did he get killed at?" Kilo asked as if he was seriously surprised.

"I heard niggahs laid in wait for him to come home and when he did they robbed him, and then flipped the house upside down looking for his stash," Smooth C replied.

"Niggah how in the fuck did you hear all of that shit?"

"Man you know how the hood be talking. Everybody be watching out of the windows until a bullet comes crashing through that motherfuckah! They say it was two niggahs hooded up in all black who did it," Smooth C added.

"How did they kill him? Did they shoot son?" Kilo asked.

"Hell yea they shot his ass, and niggahs sliced his throat from ear to ear too," Smooth C said as he demonstrated by sliding his finger across his own neck.

The two had been riding around the city all morning getting high. They had already purchased weed from three different weed spots. Kilo was behind the wheel of Smooth C's Lexus, while he played the passenger.

"It's fucked up because Flames was only thirty-five years old. He had a family and everything… I bet the niggahs who did it didn't even get no money… That's why I keep my gun on me everywhere I go. If the stick-up kids run up on me somebody is going to die on the spot!" Smooth C said before passing what was left of the blunt over to Kilo.

"Damn Smooth C, you might as well have finished the rest of that shit! I feel disrespected by you passing me some shit that small," Kilo yelled. Smooth C started laughing as he reached onto the dash board for another rolled blunt.

Kilo continued by saying, "On the real though, Flames was a foul motherfuckah Smooth C. Niggahs like him never live too long. How could you be married with two daughters, but at the same time you out here in these streets sticking dick to every fiend bitch with a pussy?"

After Smooth C finished laughing at what was obviously the truth, he admitted, "Flames was a tricking ass dude. I remember not too long ago I caught him fucking wit' the fiend bitch Sandra. She was sucking his dick in the middle of the alley. Man I started crying laughing when I saw that crazy shit."

"See what I'm saying. And Sandra looks like she got AIDS or something."

Kilo drove to another weed spot on Rosewood Terrace and went into the red brick apartment building to buy three more twenty bags of good green. It was rumored that they sold the best weed in town. Kilo had some himself but his was for sale and not for smoke.

Kilo then road to Sue's on E. Main Street to order breakfast. The restaurant was run by a Chinese husband and wife who respectfully served their customers the best morning food in Rochester. Marketview Heights was just over the bridge so many hustlers rushed to eat there every day. Kilo ordered pancakes with beef sausages, while Smooth C opted for the toast, eggs, and bacon meal. Before leaving Sue's Kilo ordered Kiki a plate to go.

"Smooth C after we take this food to your sister we need to go bag up that coke for the houses. Omar said it should be excellent cocaine because he didn't step on it at all. But even if he did; we definitely going to press it with something!" Kilo said with a smile before pulling away from the curb. He was a chemist when it came to cooking crack, and he was proud of his ability to stretch cocaine into more grams and still keep its potency.

Kilo started dealing with Smooth C recently. Being that Kay Cee was doing his own thing with the Dominicans, he focused on putting Smooth C onto how to really make money. Smooth C had shown the discipline and readiness to make a transition from a boy into a man. Kilo would just have to stay on top of him and carefully mold him into being a true hustler like himself.

Kilo gave Kiki a kiss on her forehead as he walked into the house.

"You can kiss me in front of my brother. He is not anybody," Kiki said as she playfully pushed Smooth C in his back as he passed.

"Girl mommy not here to stop me from beating your ass Kiki," Smooth C joked.

"Niggah who in the fuck you think I am? You not doing shit to my baby," Kilo said as he grabbed Kiki into his arms and gave her that long passionate kiss she wanted. Smooth C gave up and went to sit on the couch and started flipping through the channels of the TV.

"Baby Kay Cee came by here earlier acting real suspicious. He asked to use the phone after I told him you weren't here. The reason I say he was acting unusual is because normally he'd spark up a conversation or something, but today he just sat there looking all nervous. I was glad when he got the hell up out of here, for real," Kiki explained.

"Word? I wonder why he didn't call me," Kilo asked himself out loud.

"That niggah have been acting funny lately," Smooth C said from the couch. He hadn't yet told Kilo about the rumors of Kay Cee snitching that was circulating when he was locked down. He figured that Kilo would have heard the same rumors sooner or later. He didn't want to look like he was trying to create some bullshit just to get closer to Kilo.

Kilo turned in his direction, and asked, "Why you say that?"

"The man just acts weird now for no reason. I have been seeing the shit. That's why I stopped fucking with him like that," Smooth C answered.

"Shit if you look at it like that I could say you was acting differently too. Before I went to jail you wasn't pulling out guns and running niggahs off of the block in the hood... You two both are over exaggerating about Kay Cee. He's just been a little stressed out since last year when he caught that FED charge, that's all," Kilo said defensively. No one could talk bad about the friend who had killed for him.

"Say what you want baby but I know what I saw this morning. You can stick up for him all you want, but I witnessed this dude on some bullshit and I will tell him to his face," Kiki said while opening up her plate of food at the kitchen counter. "You better watch his shady ass!"

Kiki really didn't like Kay Cee because she believed he was a womanizer who swore he was a player. If it wasn't for the friendship that Kay Cee and Kilo shared then she would of told her man that his so-called homeboy tried to come on to her while he was in jail.

One day Kay Cee came over to her house and said some slick shit to her out of nowhere, like, "Don't worry Kiki because if Kilo gets convicted I'll still be here for you!" he said while licking his lips like LL Cool J. Kiki then felt so uncomfortable that she folded her arms across her chest until he left. She neglected to tell Kilo about the incident only because it was words, but if he would have touched her then he had problems.

Kilo pulled his phone from his pocket and dialed the numbers to call Kay Cee. He hung up after about five rings. "He's not answering his phone. I'll just catch up to him on the Strip... Let's roll Smooth C."

"Oh no niggah! Where are you two going so fast? You don't come in here and bounce on me like that," Kiki said with a mouth full of eggs.

Smooth C stood up and made eye contact with Kilo on the low.

"Watch me!" Kilo screamed as Smooth C hauled ass behind him towards the door.

Kiki dropped her fork onto the plate and chased behind them. When she reached the doorway she screamed, "Kilo you didn't say you loved me, you punk!"

Kilo was at the driver's door of the Lexus when he realized what she was saying, and then he ran back up onto the porch. He grabbed Kiki by the waist and kissed her softly on the cheek, and said, "I love you girl."

"I love you too Kilo. Make sure you figure out what was going on with Kay Cee. I have known him since we were kids and I'm telling you something real serious was going through his head today," Kiki said sincerely.

"Don't worry I will. Kay Cee is one of the good niggahs... Call me when you get off of work, okay? I want to take you out to dinner tonight."

"Okay. You and Cedric stay safe honey," Kiki said as she went back inside.

CHAPTER THIRTEEN
DON'T LIE

"**A** true leader must always be able to search the hearts of men. The eyes are the windows of his soul, and the mouth speaks truth or falsehood from his heart. Any man who eats from your plate and attempts to stab you in your back with the knife of deceit is not worthy of being fed. Also he must be dealt with for personal fulfillment and as an example to others who may in the future take a seat at your table..."

Reggie agreed to meet Kay Cee at Goodman Plaza this afternoon. He explained over the phone that he'd be sitting in his white Acura, with the navy blue leather rag top, at the beginning of the shopping center. Reggie was a major niggah from the cities Westside. It was him who most of the Westside hustlers purchased their crack from. He wasn't like Kilo who chose to sell cocaine from crack houses, he sold coke by weight and the lowest amount you could get from him was sixty-two grams.

Kay Cee met Reggie back in the days when he was dating his sister Monica. The two over time became good friends even though Reggie didn't like the fact that his sister was messing around with a dude from Marketview Heights. That relationship between Kay Cee and Monica later dissolved, but on the strength of the hustling game Reggie continued to do business on and off with Kay Cee over the years.

Whenever there was a drought (or shortage of cocaine) Reggie would call Kay Cee so he could get some coke from his Dominican connections. Earlier this morning; however, Kay Cee called Reggie claiming that the Dominicans didn't have any coke and that he needed to buy a brick to hold him over throughout the first of the month. "Yea I could do that for you Kay Cee. Meet me at the Goodman Plaza at two o' clock... Come alone too," Reggie said.

Benny Thompson and his fellow agent Mike Ledgeworth had been waiting in the Goodman Plaza parking lot since Kay Cee had made the phone call to Reggie. The agents had been secretly listening to every phone call Kay Cee has made in the past year. They even managed to get permission from their supervisor to tap into Kilo's home and cell phone lines. They tried very hard, but were unsuccessful in getting into Omar's phone services because they lacked certain key information about him.

Ten minutes after the phone call to Reggie the FBI agents met Kay Cee in a remote area of the city and securely taped a wire to his chest to record his conversation with Reggie. They also gave him twenty- six thousand dollars' worth of marked money to use in purchasing the cocaine from him. Before Kay Cee left the agents to meet Reggie, Benny Thompson said, "Conway, try to act normal. If you screw this one up you can kiss your freedom goodbye!"

Later, Kay Cee slowly pulled into the empty parking space next to Reggie's white Acura TL. He took a deep breath and grabbed the bag of dirty money from the passenger's seat. Before he stepped out of his Jaguar, he checked to see if his .45 caliber handgun was secure on his waist just in case shit went bad. The agents were a few parking spaces away as they began snapping numerous photos of Kay Cee and the two vehicles parked side by side from their white equipment van. Kay Cee walked around the front of the Acura avoiding eye contact with its driver. He opened the door and fell into the passenger seat.

"What's up Kay Cee? I love that money green Jaguar you

pushing. It's a good look for you playboy," Reggie said with admiration.

"Nothing much fam'. A niggah just out here trying to survive that's all... You got that key for me?" Kay Cee asked.

"Yea man you see the shit sitting right here," Reggie said with a raised brow. The white powder was tightly wrapped in plastic and had been resting on his lap the entire time in plain sight. Reggie looked over and noticed sweat starting to form on Kay Cee's forehead. For some odd reason Kay Cee was acting mighty awkward. Reggie had never seen him behave this way before. Kay Cee didn't even make any eye contact with him, he just stared straight ahead.

"Reggie, its twenty- six gees in this bag. You can count it later and call me if anything is missing," Kay Cee said with a forced smile as he looked at Reggie for the first time. *'Yea something is definitely not right with this dude,'* Reggie thought.

Reggie was just about to hand over the package when he looked to his left and for the first time noticed the suspicious looking white van parked almost four cars away. He thought nothing of it until he realized that the passenger of the van was holding up a pair of binoculars aimed in his direction. Then it all registered. *'This niggah is trying to set me up with a fucking sale!'* Reggie angrily thought. His sudden change of facial expression gave it away.

"Kay Cee, I don't know what you mean by no fucking KEY! If you were talking about drugs man you have the wrong person... I never sold drugs before in my life!" Reggie said loudly. He was talking for the hidden microphone Kay Cee could be wearing.

"What the fuck are you talking about Reggie?" Kay Cee asked confused.

"Man step the fuck out of my car, word up! I'm going to tell Kilo about this shit too niggah!" Reggie shouted.

Once Kay Cee heard Kilo's name he reached for the door handle. As he was exiting the vehicle, he said, "Reggie you tripping'. You might as well sell me that crack you have on your lap."

"Fuck you niggah. Shut my fucking door!"

Kay Cee stood in the parking lot watching Reggie speed away. He knew in his heart that this was what agent Thompson meant by blowing it...

———»«()»«———

Kilo awoke early in the morning with his right arm wrapped around Kiki's soft body. Her round ass had been pressed up against him all night. Kilo allowed his hand to make its way to caress her firm breast until he felt her nipples protruding through her silk bra. He kissed her neck as she rolled onto her back. She knew from Kilo's hardness that he wanted to have sex before he did anything else today. And her realizing that made her panties wet.

Kilo slid his hand down her stomach and under the silk fabric of her matching underwear. He slowly ran his hand along her neatly trimmed pubic hairs and softly slid his middle finger back and forth over her swelling clitoris. He could feel the love juices flowing out of her womanly opening. Kiki opened her legs for Kilo's roaming fingertips as she leaned up to reach his lips. She hurriedly pulled her panties down her thick legs, while Kilo instantly removed his boxer briefs.

The early morning sun started to beam rays of light into the spacious master bedroom. Kiki climbed over Kilo and ran her tongue down his stomach until she welcomed his erection into her mouth leading him to the back of her throat. She had become a pro at orally pleasing Kilo. She licked over his head, and then deep-throated him again. She stroked his manhood with one hand while she kept her mouth around the tip of his dick. Once she tasted a sample of his semen she knew her job was complete.

Kiki used her hand to place Kilo's throbbing dick into her hot wetness. As she began to ride him Kilo used both of his hands to spread her ass checks apart as he helped to guide her movements at the same time. She rode up and down and side to side until she reached an explosive climax. Kilo came last as he shot a heavy load deep inside of Kiki's love canal.

Kiki rested on top of Kilo for almost an hour before she got up and went downstairs to fix breakfast. Kilo looked around at the clock when Kiki left the room and noticed that it was a little after nine a.m. Usually Kilo would have been up and in the streets handling business by now. Being that today was the first of the month, he knew that money was out to be made and relaxing in bed was no way to get it.

"Kilo! Cedric is down here. He said for you to come down," Kiki screamed from the bottom to the stairs. "He claims it's important!"

Kilo lazily rose from the bed and pulled on a pair of gray Polo sweatpants, and then stretched on a black tank top.

"Kilo, last night the police hit my spot and two of yours," Smooth C reported as soon as Kilo reached the bottom of the stairs.

"What?" Kilo screamed in disbelief. Kiki stood in the kitchen listening. She didn't know what was wrong, but she could tell that Kilo wasn't happy.

"Son, Bradley and Lil' Jay are in jail."

"Wow! What time did this shit happen?" Kilo asked.

"About twelve o'clock last night, but nobody knew until early this morning when niggahs came on the block, I guess," Smooth C stated.

"Take Kiki with you to bail those niggahs out of jail. When you get back meet me on the block... I can't believe this bullshit!" Kilo said as he ran back upstairs.

About a half of an hour later they all left the house. Smooth C and Kiki headed downtown for the County Jail, while Kilo hopped in Kiki's Benz destined for the hood to check on his drug houses.

When Kilo pulled up in front of his twenty spot he noticed that green stickers were posted on all to the front windows. He knew from experience that the police left those stickers on the house to notify the community that drugs were being sold out of the apartment. This was the spot that Lil' Jay was working last night. Kilo then rode around the corner to find that his weight house was also decorated with the police's neon green stickers. "Damn!" Kilo yelled. He was upset because he had left a half of a key, weighed up with Shaun so that he wouldn't have to keep running back and forth into the city every time the house ran out of work. The good thing about it was that Smooth C didn't say that Shaun was in jail too, so he must have gotten away when the police busted the house last night. However, Shaun didn't call him yet and that was kind of weird.

Kilo slowly cruised down the Strip looking for Shaun. He noticed a group of familiar hustlers huddled up together on the corner. When he rolled by Shaun stepped away from the crowd to flag him down. Kilo pulled over and waited for Shaun to get in.

"Kilo son the police hit the spot last night! The only reason I got away was because I fucked around and leaped out the window. The boys chased me for about fifteen minutes until I left they ass by Central Park," Shaun explained. He was tall and skinny. He was the type of person who demonstrated with their hands while talking.

"So what happened to all of the work?" Kilo asked.

"Shit happened so fast… By the time I realized they were coming it was too late. So I just left everything on the table and bounced."

"You didn't sell any of the coke before they came?" Kilo asked when he noticed that Shaun hadn't attempted to hand over any money.

"Nah… I didn't get a chance to sell nothing. It was mad slow," Shaun said.

"So you mean to tell me that from seven o'clock until twelve nobody came to the spot, right?" Kilo asked.

"Nah Kilo, nobody came… For real," Shaun answered.

In that amount of time the entire amount of crack usually had been sold by then. The house was bubbling. Plus Kilo himself sent two people their personally to buy large quantities of cocaine last night at around ten o'clock. *'This niggah is trying to play me. He probably left some of the coke in the house, but this motherfuck-ah sold something before the police came,'* Kilo thought. He then looked down at Shaun's left pocket and it was bulging.

"You sure?" Kilo asked again.

"Yea, I wouldn't lie to you Kilo," Shaun pleaded.

"Step out of the car for a second Shaun," Kilo said.

Shaun opened the door and stood on the sidewalk thinking that Kilo was buying his bullshit story about not having any money to give him at all. While Kilo was getting out he pulled the chrome .38 special from his inside coat pocket. Shaun didn't notice the pistol until Kilo came around the back of the black Benz with it clutched in his right hand.

"Kilo what's up man, that's my word..." Before Shaun could get the next set of lies off the tip of his tongue Kilo smacked the shit out of him with the barrow of his gun. Shaun's face immediately started leaking blood as he dropped down to his knees. "Please Kilo don't kill me!"

Kilo ignored his cries and continued to beat blood from his head with the butt of his revolver.

Someone from across the street yelled, "Look, Kilo over there fucking Shaun up!" Soon a small crowd had formed around as Kilo relentlessly pounded the man who he felt was stealing from him.

Shaun tried to block each vicious blow with his hands as he screamed for help. Kilo went into Shaun's pockets and pulled out a stack of money. All of a sudden the kid was able to walk around with stacks on deck, but two months ago he was broke as hell. Losing the money wasn't the problem for Kilo; it was the fact that Shaun was lying that infuriated him the most.

"When you lie to a real niggah this is what you get motherfuck-ah. Because of me the whole hood is bubbling, and you have the nerve to try and beat me out of a few dollars?" Kilo asked as he back handed Shaun in the face.

"Kilo you're going to kill the boy if you keep beating him like that," a young woman wearing a blue scarf around her head reasoned.

At her words Kilo smashed Shaun's brown face in one last time. He walked towards the terrified crowd with his gun still in hand, and then he threw the money he retrieved from Shaun's pocket onto the ground before them.

"I'm a true hustler," Kilo said. "I will never sell my soul for a few punk ass dollars!"

Kilo watched as the hungry and excited hustlers fought over every dollar scattered on the ground as he jumped back into the Benz and quietly sped away from the curb. Shaun was lying unconscious on the sidewalk floating in a pool of his own blood.

CHAPTER FOURTEEN
SAME ASS NIGGAH

"Let no amount of money, pressure, or material gains change the overall person you have always been. When you're doing badly; people are going to talk bad about you. When you're doing well, they'll have something to say about that. Even during hard times you must be patient and always act the same as you would in a comfortable condition. To some people change is the universal sign of weakness..."

Tonya came out of the bathroom wearing a light blue set of bra and thongs. She was tall and thick in all of the right places. Her brown skin covered her body like warm caramel. Kay Cee had been sleeping with her on and off for about three years now. Lately he began to treat her special because she was six months pregnant with his first child. Tonya was overwhelmed by his sudden invitation for her to relax in the Hyatt for a couple days. Tonya was a cool female to know, but she was also gullible and obeyed Kay Cee's every demand.

Kay Cee had been laying low at the Hyatt Hotel in downtown Rochester. He had yet to see or hear from the irritating FBI agents since the unsuccessful buy from Reggie in Goodman Plaza. He didn't even know whether or not to consider himself officially on the run. But he did know that if the agents didn't contact him first, then he wouldn't be so eager to reach them either. Since checking into the hotel with Tonya, his phone remained off. This morning was the first time it was turned back on. He didn't want to make it seem like he was hiding from the FBI. He just needed a few days to let shit die down so he could put things into their proper perspectives. Kay Cee was coping with the fact that this whole situation was turning for the worse.

Another reason it took Kay Cee so long to turn his phone back on was that he didn't want to speak to Kilo. He wasn't sure if Reggie had caught up to him and ran his mouth about what happened the other day. He would hate to kill Reggie, but the way things were looking now he'd have to before Reggie could spread that bullshit all over the town.

"Daddy what's the matter? You don't look like you're in a good mood this morning. Can I do something to make you feel better?" Tonya asked as she climbed on the bed.

"I'm peace baby. Just a little stressed," Kay Cee responded.

"Do you want to talk about it? You know after I have the baby I want to use my degree to get a job as a counselor... Let me practice on you?" she asked.

"Girl I would have to kill your pretty ass if I was to spill my guts to you," Kay Cee said with a smile, but he was dead serious though. He would really have to kill anybody who knew his current secrets. Even his soon to be baby mother couldn't be trusted with knowing that he was indulging in the wickedest part of the game...snitching!

"Boy it can't be that serious. I'm here to make things better, not just for you to fuck my brains out all weekend. Can I do anything else for you?" Tonya asked while rubbing her hand in a circular motion over his stomach.

"Yea, first you can pass me that blunt from the ashtray."

Tonya got onto her knees and bent forward off of the bed to reach the ashtray while flashing Kay Cee with a beautiful view of the heart shape that her ass formed in the meantime. He slowly caressed it while she was bent over in that arousing position.

"Oh I know what you want now niggah," she said while shaking her head from side to side as she passed him his blunt. Kay Cee used a lighter to spark it, and then he exhaled a series of circles that disappeared in seconds.

"And what's that you future psychologist?" Kay Cee asked before she grabbed a hold of his dick through his boxers. "Oh yea, you are definitely on the right track Tonya."

The couple had already had sex all over the luxury suite over and over again, from the bubbling hot tub to the huge bed. But her pregnant pussy was so good that he couldn't have enough. Tonya stroked his manhood gently until it grew in her small hand. She then positioned herself between his legs and welcomed his throbbing shaft into her mouth. While she was sucking on his dick, Kay Cee's cell phone rung for the first time in two days. He reached over onto the night stand and grabbed it. He looked at the caller ID display and was glad to see that it wasn't Kilo or the FBI. "Hello?"

"Kay Cee baby this is Tina. I've been trying to call for the last couple of days. I even rode through the Heights twice looking for you yesterday. Where have you been?" she asked in a concerned tone.

"I went on a vacation to Philly. I just got back this morning," Kay Cee said. Tonya looked up when she heard him lie to the person on the other end of the line, then she went back to sucking his dick.

"I miss you. When can I see you again?" Tina asked.

"I don't know. I'm kind of busy… Hold on for one second T-." Kay Cee clicked over to answer the other line, "Hello?"

"What's up niggah? Where in the fuck have you been lately? You got me calling you all crazy like I'm one of your bitches or something," Kilo snapped.

"I've been on the run around. I was meaning to get with you fam', but you know how shit gets sometimes."

"Well I need to see you, soon! You've been missing in action and shit niggah… I really don't want to talk over this phone because my shit has been acting funny. My house phone too… So when you plan on coming through the hood?" Kilo asked.

"Sometimes today I'll slide through there for sure."

"I'll be up there." Kilo said before hanging up.

Kay Cee switched back over to Tina, but she had already disconnected because he had her on hold too long.

"Who was that?" Tonya asked as she shifted onto her back beside Kay Cee to take off her thongs. Sucking on his dick had made her extremely horny.

"That was Kilo. He was kind of worried about me because he hasn't seen me in a couple of days," Kay Cee replied without mentioning anything about one of his other whores, Tina, who had called also. He pulled off his boxers and exposed his erection.

"Why did you tell Kilo you were out of town?" she asked.

"I told you I didn't need counseling… I need some of this pussy," Kay Cee said as he slid his hand between her wet legs.

Tonya smiled and climbed on top of Kay Cee. She started riding him backwards while arching her back to meet his thrusts into her. Kay Cee slapped her soft ass cheeks as hard as he could when her movements began feeling too good on him. Even though she was pregnant their sex remained ruff. With both hands he squeezed the sides of her waist to pull her back while forcing his manhood up her love canal. Tonya screamed from the pleasure as she bounced up and down, and back in forth onto Kay Cee. Her pussy was wet and tight, but he couldn't really enjoy it like he wanted too because there was way too much other shit going on in his life.

'What did Kilo mean when he said his phones were acting funny?' Kay Cee thought. Then one of the craziest thoughts he ever had in his life crossed his frustrated mind, 'I might have to smoke Kilo ass too.'

Kay Cee tossed Tonya onto her back and forcefully held her legs up high in the air. He attempted to relieve his pain, anger, and stress by pounding and slamming his dick deep into her pussy as hard as he possibly could. Tonya's cries and screams of pleasure was exactly what he felt like doing inside, except his pain would come from the rage of falling too deep into the life of a hustler.

Kilo had already sold almost five grand worth of crack while he stood on the block waiting for Kay Cee. It wasn't his intentions to come in the Heights to sell drugs today, but whenever he was around he inadvertently cut everybody else's throat. If a fiend came on the Strip looking to get high Kilo would point them in the direction to one of his spots where he sold bags. And if a hustler wanted to buy some grams he would take them to his new weight house around the corner.

Even though Kilo rarely posted up on the Strip niggahs still hated when he did because most of their money automatically stopped while he was on the block. You would see hustlers getting inside their cars and leaving the hood until Kilo was gone. The only reason he was standing on the block so long today in the cool September weather was because of Kay Cee. He needed to speak with him in order to figure out where his mind was at. It was unlike Kay Cee to stay away from the hood days at a time without contacting him. When Kilo talked to Kay Cee this morning it was eleven a.m., and now it was a quarter past four in the afternoon.

A black Honda Prelude pulled up to the curb in front of Kilo. He bent down to try and look through the heavily tinted windows to see who was inside. The passenger's window slowly lowered and revealed the identity of a light-skinned female whom Kilo didn't recognize.

"What's good ma'?" Kilo asked.

"Hi handsome. We was riding past, and my home girl wanted to stop and holla' at you. Hope you don't mind," she said leaning back so that Kilo could see the drivers face. They were both pretty as hell.

It was nothing unusual for women to stop and try to get on with one of the many hustlers who posted up on the Strip daily. Especially now that Kilo had the entire hood getting some type of paper. Females from all over the R.O.C were trying to get a niggah from Marketview Heights. To them it was like having an expensive Gucci purse to show off and brag about to their jealous friends.

The Heights was always known for being a place that money circulated since the early eighties, before crack even hit Rochester hard. Hustlers then sold strictly powder cocaine to mostly white collar costumers. But now all of the old niggahs who had it back then were either dead or in jail. The fate of a hustler back then didn't change at all from how it was in today's drug game. Kilo outdid all of the old legends. He made it to where anybody from the hood could actually be somebody if they wanted too. It was a known fact that every female wanted a baller; even the so-called good girls. And there should've been a bulletin board posted up for them that read: *Ladies if you're looking for a true hustler ride through Marketview Heights!*

"Hi sexy," the driver said to Kilo with a smile. She was also light complexioned, and she had her hair going to the back in small braids like MC Lyte. From Kilo's view she looked like a petite woman with not too much ass, if any.

"My name is Kilo, and yours?" he asked as he walked up to them and rested both of his hands on the top of the car.

"Kilo!" the passenger shouted in disbelief. Kilo was wearing a brown waist length fur coat with a black du-rag tied over his braids. "You're not the Kilo that everybody in the town is talking about."

Kilo smiled at her ignorance, "Why not, because I'm not wearing platinum chains and diamond watches? That shit only makes niggahs like me super-hot!"

Both girls laughed at his logic. "We know you the man and you're the reason most of these niggahs are getting paid. We just heard so much about you and never expected to meet you in person," the passenger confessed. Kilo really liked her, but he didn't want to violate the driver. He wanted the passenger because she was the voice of the two and more aggressive than her friend.

"So what are your names?" Kilo asked as he noticed Kay Cee

bending the corner. He parked on the side street behind the rented Grand Am G6 Kilo was driving.

"My name is Fay, and this is my peoples Star," the passenger said while leaning back and pointing to the driver again.

"Fay, my man Kay Cee just pulled up. I think he'll be feeling you. You two should let us take you out tonight and show you a good time?" Kilo offered.

Star and Fay turned in their seats as they watched Kay Cee getting out of his car. The first thing Fay noticed was the huge twenty-four inch chrome rims on his Jaguar. She smiled when she saw that he was a light-skinned pretty boy with a diamond chain glistering over his chest. Kay Cee was certainly her type of niggah.

Kay Cee walked up and slapped Kilo a five, and then he asked, "Who are these beautiful ladies?"

"This is Fay, and the shy one over there name is Star," Kilo answered.

"I'm not shy," Star said defensively.

"Well get out of the car so I could see how you really look," Kilo challenged.

Star slid from behind the steering wheel and onto the street. Before she got around the car Kilo thought to himself, *'Damn she's going to be short and skinny too.'* But when she finally came around the back of her Honda both Kay Cee and Kilo's mouths dropped. You could actually see the knot of her pussy sitting in the middle of her thick thighs. She was wearing a pair of pink leggings with a white tee shirt. Her upper body was small, but she was perfect everywhere else. Kilo was now glad that he didn't pass this one up, because Star was sexy as hell.

"Boy you know it is cold out here, right?" Star asked as she folded her arms across her small chest.

"Kilo she's a nice one," Kay Cee said in his ear as he walked to the passenger's side of the Honda to talk to Fay.

"So are you going to let us take you and Fay out tonight?" Kilo asked again.

"Yea, we don't have anything else going on later... I know you have a girlfriend though," Star said.

"The way I'll treat you tonight Star you'll never care if I had a woman or not. What me and you do will stay between us- I mean, if you could accept that!"

"I respect it Kilo. And believe me for you being honest I won't hold anything back from you, okay?" Star asked.

Kilo talked to Star for almost ten minutes before she complained again about the weather. He walked her to the driver's door and gave her a long hug.

"Alright. We'll definitely see you two tonight and get into something real special," Kilo said before the two beautiful ladies pulled off.

Kilo then turned to Kay Cee.

"So what's up my niggah?" Kay Cee asked.

"You... I see you've been on the low lately. What's that all about?"

"Man this ankle bracelet shit is crazy. Lately the FEDs have been pressuring me to obey my curfew. But when you called this morning I was at the hotel fucking with Tonya's crazy ass," Kay Cee said.

"You still fuck with that crazy ass bitch?" Kilo asked.

"Niggah be easy, she is about to have my seed," Kay Cee said semi-seriously.

"Oh yea I forgot. No disrespect playboy," Kilo said with a soft punch to Kay Cee's right shoulder. "So what's happening with your case?"

"Shit. They still don't know what they want to do yet. I'll be glad when this shit is finally over though," Kay Cee said as he lit the blunt that was behind his ear.

Kilo was watching his actions carefully; even while they were talking to Fay and Star he was observing Kay Cee's every move. He wasn't acting weird at all. Kilo couldn't figure out what it was that made Kiki and Smooth C say that he was acting strange.

"Son, we need to scoop those two bad ass bitches up tonight for sure!" Kay Cee said excitedly. Talking to Fay before he had the chance to speak with Kilo helped him feel more comfortable. When he first pulled up and saw Kilo he was nervous as hell. Everything felt the same so it was easy for Kay Cee to act normal.

"Oh without a question we will. Star's short ass was thick as fuck. I'm going to hurt that pussy tonight if she gives it up," Kilo said. "But on some other shit Kay Cee- do you be hearing funny noises on any of your phones? It sounds like someone is on the three way listening or something."

Smooth C floated past the corner heading in the direction of the bridge. He blew his horn twice as he passed Kilo and Kay Cee in his Lexus. They both shot up their right fists in the air to acknowledge him. Then Kay Cee answered by saying, "Nah fam', I don't be hearing no unusual shit on my phones."

"Do you think the FBI could be tapping into our phone lines?"

"Shit Kilo, the FEDs are the FEDs. They do shit like that, son. That's why I don't call you too much and when I do it's never about business. I'm not saying your phones aren't tapped, but knowing my situation, who knows what those crackers trying to do."

As soon as Kay Cee said that Kilo's cell phone started ringing. He pulled it from his hip, and then made eye contact with Kay Cee. They both started laughing. After Kilo answered, he turned his back to Kay Cee and walked a few steps away while he talked to Kiki.

When Kilo came back, he said, "That was Kiki. She needs for me to go to Rent-A-Center with her to pick out a dining room set... So at about nine o'clock tonight we'll pick up those chicks and see if we can get it poppin'!"

"Okay Kilo. I'll see you then, call me... Nah fuck that shit, just meet me up here," Kay Cee said jokingly.

Kay Cee and Kilo walked across the street to their respective vehicles. Kay Cee was feeling a lot better after talking to Kilo, but he still couldn't tell if he knew anything yet. Kilo was sharp enough in the head to be able to conceal the way he was really feeling about a certain situation. Kay Cee knew that sooner or later the whole shit would come to light, unless of' course he could zip Reggie up in a black bag first...

CHAPTER FIFTEEN
PLEASURE BEFORE
BUSINESS

"**N**o matter what you're doing in life or how bad things are going at the moment always make sure you find time to enjoy yourself. It's nothing wrong with putting things off in order to have a little fun. We only have one life to live, and just like we endure the pain we must embrace happiness as well. But after the excitement dies down you have to get back on your job, if you want to stay on top..."

They all sat quietly in a small apartment just outside of Marketview Heights. Two men were in the kitchen rolling up blunts from a pound of hash weed that was spread all over the table. The two young females who they brought with them were patiently waiting in the living room. The only source of light was being supplied by the small television before them.

Somehow these young ladies ended up here with these crazy ass niggahs. They had been listening and observing the men conversations all night. They expected to be wined and dined tonight since these niggahs claimed to be from Marketview Heights. Instead the women were made to feel very uncomfortable and upset that they decided to chill with these weird dudes.

The girls nervously watched the big gorilla looking niggah hold up some type of machine gun. Since they had gotten there all the two dudes did was smoke weed and clean their guns. They had the arsenal of a small army. The smaller man of the two was short, brown-skinned, and he had a deformed right hand. Later the girls would find out that his hand had gotten fucked up after being shot five times. He was guzzling a bottle of Hennessey like it was Gatorade.

Foxy was a young seventeen year old girl from F.I.G.H.T Village. She was dark in complexion, and looked similar to the female rapper Foxy Brown. She was a beautiful chick, but her troubled childhood led her to putting herself in ugly situations with older men. Her friend and she met Steal and his off the wall boy Black earlier at the corner store in her hood. When they first met Steal and his accomplice they both seemed cool until they got drunk and started playing with those damn guns.

The big black niggah with the long scar on his face had introduced himself as Steal. He was angry about something, and it became apparent once the alcohol entered his system. All he kept saying was, "That motherfuckah think he slick. I got a trick for his ass."

Foxy wanted to leave but her home girl was getting drunk with Black and she was starting to act stupid also. Foxy knew she couldn't leave her alone because she was only fifteen and there would be no telling what she'd let them do to her without anyone there to say, "That's enough!" The fifteen your old was matching Black drink for drink, and blunt for blunt as the night went on. Foxy smoked a few blunts herself but refused to get drunk with them. If there wasn't so many loaded weapons lying around or if the house was a little cleaner, then she would have probably drunk with her friend and maybe she would of sucked and fucked too.

"That niggah sent me on a bullshit mission Black," Steal said as he stood next to the TV. "When he's the niggah we should've robbed. He knew that motherfuckah Flames was broke!"

The liquor and weed made Steal furious. The more he drunk and smoked the more he ran his mouth recklessly in front of Foxy and her home girl. He was so intoxicated that he'd never remember all of the shit he said. His roll dog was equally as dumb because he didn't warn Steal to watch what he was saying around the bitches they had just met.

"Kilo will feel the pain of every last one of these bullets," Steal said while slamming a clip into a black .380 handgun. "He would rather look out for them coward ass niggahs on the block when I was the one knocking niggahs out for him in jail!"

After Kilo told Steal that Flames was buying bricks of cocaine, Steal drove to Buffalo and got his man Black, who he had met in prison. Black was supposed to have been robbing mad niggahs in the Ruff Buff, and it was vouched for by a lot of gangsters that knew him from the streets. He didn't hesitate to join Steal once he learned that the robbery had the potential of so much money. Plus Steal said in exaggeration that it was possible they could get as many as ten kilograms of crack. It sounded so easy that Black couldn't resist. But of' course shit didn't go quite the way Steal planned it. They came up empty handed, and had to kill Flames in the process. So now they turned their attention to the man himself. They began to secretly follow Kilo everywhere he went for the last two weeks, and now Steal knew that he lived out in Webster, New York with his girlfriend. And that's where he figured Kilo's stash had to be, and if it wasn't, then his heart surely was.

Black pulled Foxy's friend from the couch and led her into a dark corner of the living room. She dropped to her young knees and started sucking his dick, while Steal advised, "Enjoy that head niggah because soon the pleasure will be over, and then it's strictly business in the R.O.C!"

Steal placed his gun and a half empty bottle of Remy Martin on the small wooden table, and then slowly walked over and stood in front of Foxy, who was still seated on the couch. She was watching her drunken friend sucking the shit out of Black's dick. Without saying a word to her Steal unzipped his pants and let his long erection hang down in front of her face. Foxy thought about it for a second, and then she reluctantly grabbed it into her small hand and forced it deeply into her mouth.

After having a great time together the happy foursome pulled into the parking lot of the Comfort Inn Hotel. They ate dinner at a discreet upscale restaurant in the suburb of Brighton. Later the two couples just rode around in Kay Cee's Jaguar talking and enjoying the quiet sceneries. Star and Fay felt like queens as their dates spent hundreds of dollars to make sure they enjoyed themselves.

At dinner the two women excused themselves from the table. Once inside the bathroom they planned to show Kilo and Kay Cee a good time before the night was over.

"These niggahs are so down to earth," Star admitted as she looked in the mirror at her make-up to see if there were any flaws.

"Tell me about it girl. Kay Cee is spending money on me like it grows on trees or something," Fay returned.

"I'll be so mad if they just drop us off without trying to get some pussy because I'm definitely not telling Kilo no!"

"I know that's right. We can go straight to the hotel from here for all I care," Fay said in agreement.

Meanwhile, Kilo and Kay Cee were discussing similar plans at the table.

"Kilo Fay isn't that bad, huh?" Kay Cee asked.

"She's alright. I'll fuck with her son... Where should we take them when we leave here? We just can't drop them off at home and call it a night. Star's been all over me. I know she ready to fuck!" Kilo said.

"Let's go to that Comfort Inn we passed on the highway. It's nice in there," Kay Cee suggested. Moments later they were pulling up in front of the hotel.

There was no question that everybody was on the same page. It was almost guaranteed to be a whole lot of rough sex in the air tonight. Fay had turned out to be a little on the slim side, but Kay Cee was still feeling her because she had a nice personality. She also possessed some beautiful hazel eyes that were slanted to the point of questioning her nationality. Kay Cee couldn't help but to get lost in her gaze a few times over dinner.

Kilo chose the suburb of Brighton to eat because nobody he knew from the city ever visited there. It turned out to be an excellent decision because Star couldn't keep her hands off of him. She even tried to kiss him once at dinner, but he quickly turned his face and welcomed her to his cheek. Kilo wasn't much of a kisser. He only would kiss Kiki occasionally.

Before heading to the hotel Kay Cee stopped at a well-known bootlegger that was located just on the city limits. Kilo hopped out and went in to buy a gallon of Gin. He was hoping to get some dark liquor like Remy Martin or Hennessey, but Gin was all that the old man had left. Kilo already had a half-pound of weed that he brought especially for this date. He could tell by looking at Fay's dark lips earlier that she was a weed smoker.

It had been a while since Kilo and Kay Cee were with two women on a date like this. It wasn't anything new to them because they've been doing this shit for years now. They even had codes for different situations. Like, when one of them said, "Live and direct," it meant that they felt like the chicks they had could be fucked in the same room together. But occasionally, depending on the class of the women they'd be forced to call, "Solo treatment," meaning that separate rooms would be required in order for both of them to get some pussy. Kilo and Kay Cee knew from experience that certain females were freaks, but for some reasons they wouldn't suck a dick in front of their home girls. However, tonight anything was possible, and the call was, "Live and direct."

The double bed room was big and extremely spacious. There were two queen-sized beds side by side, and a burgundy love seat against the far wall. The green carpet was as soft as cotton and felt like you were floating on air when you walked across it. The tall floor lamp in the corner perfectly illuminated the room to the effect that no extra lighting was needed.

As soon as Kay Cee turned on the TV that was attached to the wall in front of the beds, the sounds of a woman screaming filled the room. A black man was on the screen slamming his self harshly into a small white woman from behind. "Keep it there Kay Cee," Fay begged as her and Star removed their coats and shoes.

Kilo sat on the comfortable love seat and began to roll big blunts from the zip-lock bag, while Fay and Star each sat on a separate bed watching the porno movie; both smiling.

"Can I roll one Kilo?" Fay asked. Kilo hesitated before taking out a crisp ten dollar bill, folding it in half, and then filling the bill with two big buds of lime green weed.

"You sure you know how to twist Fay? We only got two boxes of Phillies for the night," Kilo asked as he passed her the weed.

"Boy please, I smoke weed every day!"

"She's not lying either," Star added as if her friend smokes too much.

Everybody was enjoying themselves. They were laughing at each other's jokes, and slowly sipping on their cups of Gin & Juice as blunts rotated around in a circle. It was like old times between Kilo and Kay Cee as they sat together on the love seat smoking blunt after blunt, and at the same time entertaining Fay and Star with their cool conversations.

Once the alcohol began to work in Kay Cee's system he started to feel emotional. He couldn't help but to think about the pain he was going to cause Kilo once shit hit the fan. He had forgotten how cool and caring Kilo could be. They were just alike in so many ways. They both came from the slums, and in many people eyes, they rose. They both loved females with a passion and lived to make money. Their brotherly love had kept them close for a long time. Kay Cee felt like shit knowing that he was the one folding under the pressures associated with the game.

Kay Cee glanced over at Kilo who was busy laughing at Star's story about her broke ass baby father. Kay Cee thought, *'I violated the trust of a real niggah who loved me like a brother. I deserve to die for the shit I did.'* Only being drunk could bring a man to the brink of these feelings. Although he would never tell Kilo this was how he really felt deep inside.

It was beginning to get late. Everybody was high and drunk as hell. The XXX rated flick had been playing all night. But they were so wrapped up in each other's company that they paid it little attention. Now that the conversation and laughter had faded the sounds of rough sex coming from the television refilled the room.

Kilo climbed in the bed with Star. Kay Cee and Fay were already half sleep in the other bed. Kilo reached over and turned the lamp off leaving the only sound and light coming from the TV.

Once Star felt that Kilo was in the bed with her she rolled onto her back. She wanted Kilo to fuck her doggy style just like they were doing in the XXX movie. She was on fire from listening to the woman screaming and the sounds of their flesh meeting each other's bodies. Kilo slowly worked his hand down to Star's wet pussy. He was dying to touch it ever since he saw her on the block earlier today. He could feel her moistness through her tight spandex pants. She spread her legs apart to give him a better opportunity to feel her.

Fay was secretly watching them out of the corner of her eyes as she played with her hot pussy next to Kay Cee. After her hormones became uncontrollable, she got out of the bed and started taking off her clothes. When she stood up the room was spinning from the effects of the alcohol. Kilo watched as each piece of Fay's clothing fell onto the carpet floor, while he plunged his fingers in and out of Star's soaked womanhood. The last article of clothes Kilo saw hit the floor was her purple thongs. Fay's body was exceptionally curvaceous for a slim woman. Her nipples were round and dark, and she had a bush of pubic hairs on her pussy that ran off onto her thighs. *'Kay Cee has to be sleep,'* Kilo thought.

"Kay Cee! Niggah wake the fuck up… Live and direct you drunk motherfuckah!" Kilo yelled.

Fay and Star both started laughing. They all knew that Kay Cee was drunk as hell because they were feeling it too. "Shhh-," Fay said to Kilo with her index finger over her lips. "I'll wake him up."

Fay climbed back onto the bed and started unzipping Kay Cee's pants. Kilo and Star both undressed in the bed and tossed their clothes on the floor. Fay pulled out Kay Cee's hard-on and started sucking on it slowly while he was still asleep. Star took the Lifestyle condom from Kilo, and then used her mouth to roll it down his dick.

When Kay Cee finally woke up moments later his wet dick was still in Fay's hand, and she was smiling at his amazed expression. When he looked over to the other bed Kilo was on top of Star fucking her brains out. Kilo and Kay Cee made eye contact and smiled just like they did back in the days while fucking two bitches in the same room.

"You a crazy ass niggah Kilo," Kay Cee said as he began to undress.

CHAPTER SIXTEEN
STRICTLY BUSINESS

"It should never be personal when the business calls for action. Leave your emotions out of situations you didn't create. A person who wants to be successful in his field knows when to put an end to the deceit, untrustworthiness, and disloyalty. This is just as much a part of the business as the work is itself..."

Kilo was furious as he read the letter given to him by Reggie's sister, Monica. She had waited on the Strip all afternoon until she finally saw Kilo ride past. She flagged him down and personally delivered the letter from jail just as her brother asked.

"How could this shit be true?" Kilo yelled as he sat inside of a rental car on a side street in the hood. He kept reading one particular sentence over and over again: *"Kilo I swear to God your man Kay Cee set me up!"* Reggie wrote.

Apparently, Reggie was being held in Batavia, New York at the federal holding center on a sealed indictment by the FBI. A week ago he and five other co-defendants he did business with were arrested. The FBI, ATF, and the RPD Drug Enforcement officers served warrants in several different locations in a six month indictment. The drug bust yielded twelve handguns, four kilograms of crack cocaine, and more than 1.5 million dollars in cash.

Reggie claimed in his letter to Kilo that the FBI had a confidential informant who was still on the streets, and that he was positive it was Kay Cee. He also described the events that happened at Goodman Plaza when Kay Cee tried to set him up. He wrote to Kilo that his lawyer told him that the FBI has audio evidence of an undercover attempt to sell crack cocaine, and named Goodman Plaza as the location.

In the brief letter Reggie insinuated that he was going to kill Kay Cee as soon as he made bail. But this was way too personal for Kilo to allow anyone else to have that pleasure. Reggie's letter answered all of Kilo's questions. It explained why he saw Kay Cee riding in the back seat of a suspicious car with two shady looking men a week ago. Kilo didn't pay it much attention because of the black dude sitting in the passenger seat. However, Kiki was the first one to spot them at the intersection of Clinton Avenue and Clifford, and knowing her she went to saying shit like, "His ass probably riding with the police," and "You never know what that niggah up to Kilo. Something's just not right with Kay Cee anymore." Kilo quickly took up for Kay Cee by telling her that the two men probably was Kay Cee's clientele.

The letter also explained the noises on his phones, and why his drug houses were getting raided by police so fast. Kay Cee was the only one who knew about certain shit. He knew about things that would leave Kilo vulnerable if he had become weak enough to cooperate with the FEDs. *'How could I have been so fucking naive?'* Kilo thought. *'I should have listened to Omar, Kiki, and Smooth C when they were trying to warn me about this niggah!'*

Kilo's pride was at its breaking point. He felt disrespected and now there was something to prove in order to hold onto to his ego. There was no telling what Kay Cee had already told the FEDs, Kilo reasoned. There was no question in his mind that Kay Cee had to die a painful and sudden death for his unforgivable betrayal.

Kilo had been waiting in the bushes for hours, and finally it was about to happen. The moment he anticipated was now casually walking into sight. Kay Cee was coming around the corner drinking from a Corona bottle. Kilo crouched down lower in his position so he would definitely be out of sight, until the perfect time. Kilo made sure that he found a hiding place directly across from the only corner store on the Strip.

The Mini Mart was the local hang out for all of the Marketview Heights drug dealers, crack heads, and prostitutes. Usually this corner always had at least ten people standing around doing something illegal. However, tonight was rather odd. It was 10:30 p.m. on a Friday night and the corner was dead, except for a wino named Stew.

Kay Cee walked past Stew on his way into the store. After he passed, Stew looked him up and down, and then he muttered, "Faggot." Luckily Kay Cee didn't hear him because he'd of easily had gotten ass kicking number five thousand.

Stew was the type of drunk who had been knocked out by damn near everybody living in Marketview Heights. He even called some females "bitches" before and they beat his ass. But no matter how many times he got his ass whooped, once a sip of alcohol was in his system you were bound to get cursed out.

Kilo knew that out of all places, here is where he'd catch Kay Cee slipping. At least once a day every hustler and local resident came to the corner store. It was like the central headquarters of the hood. No hustler parked their cars directly on the Strip so Kilo knew that Kay Cee was parked around the corner on one of the many side streets in the Heights. For a moment Kilo contemplated rushing around the corner to hide somewhere by Kay Cee's car, then he reasoned that would probably be too much moving around, jumping fences, and hiding his distinct walk from people. He decided to just wait; good things are bound to happen when you exhibit patience.

Kay Cee came out of the store looking both ways before opening another bottle of Corona. Using a lighter he flipped off the top and guzzled the popular beer until the back of his throat started to hurt. Stew was staring at him the entire time he had the bottle tilted to his face. He was dying for one sip.

"What the fuck are you looking at Stew?" Kay Cee shouted.

"Let me drink with you? Young punk…" Stew said demandingly, but also with a desperate facial expression.

"I'll think about it," Kay Cee said as he began to crack open a Phillies blunt. He dumped the contents onto the concrete, licked the remaining blunt paper, and passed the Corona to Stew after guzzling most of it. Stew's eyes lit up like a Christmas tree once the bottle was in his hand.

"Now get your drunken ass off of the block. You are making me hot. I know you see those camera's up on the corner motherfuckah?" Kay Cee shouted. Stew turned and walked away while mumbling something under his breath.

Kilo watched from the bushes as Kay Cee dumped a bag of weed onto the blunt paper and started breaking the buds into fine crumbs with his fingers.

Kay Cee constantly looked back and forth down the Strip. He was on the lookout for the police and potential customers. He had five eight balls in his pocket that he wanted to sell before heading to the club. The money would add to his pocket change and later be spent on alcohol and women.

A group of females loudly walked past the bushes that Kilo was hiding in. One female yelled across the street, saying, "Hi Kay Cee!"

He yelled back, "What's up! Liz make sure you don't go anywhere tonight because I'm coming over after the club."

"Gayle said where Kilo at," she asked on behalf of her thick light-skinned friend walking with her. "She's staying at my house tonight so if you see Kilo tell him to come over with you!"

"Okay, I'll call him later to see if he's busy."

The Strip returned to its original serenity as the females turned the corner towards Liz's apartment building.

After Kay Cee finished rolling his blunt he stuffed it behind his ear. Kilo watched as he walked towards the side of the store loosening his pants. Kay Cee made a left into the small parking lot adjacent to the store. The parking lot was designated for the Spanish owner who drove a burgundy Mustang.

Kilo pulled a black bandana with white designs over his face and tied a knot on the back of his head. He discreetly emerged from the bushes and onto the sidewalk. Kilo knew exactly what Kay Cee was going behind the Mini Mart to do, and his patience was about to pay off because there would be no better time than now.

Wearing black clothing from head to toe, Kilo jogged across the two lane street. Looking both ways as he crossed he made a mental note of everything that was on the Strip. Amazingly there was nothing to interfere with the dangerous task at hand. It was one that required no mistakes. Nobody was standing around, no occupied cars were parked along the street, and most importantly there was no police in sight. Kilo wasn't worried about the cameras on the corner because they always dispatched police after shit was over.

Entering the parking lot just seconds behind Kay Cee, Kilo pulled out a chrome nine millimeter from his waist, and then he slid it into the front pouch of his hooded sweatshirt. He thought of turning around as his heart began to race. But principle was principle and he only knew one way to skin a rat, and that was by hot bullets from a huge automatic weapon. The real reason for his sudden anxiety was the fact that Kay Cee was like a brother, and now his lack of morals, loyalty, and self-pride was surely about to get him killed.

Kilo took a deep breath before he turned behind the store. It was extremely dark. The only illumination came from a light post on a side street that was able to shine over a small house next to the store. Kay Cee had his back turned and was in the exact spot where Kilo knew he would be. He was in a corner taking a piss. Relieving himself must of felt real good because Kay Cee had his eyes closed and his head tilted back as if he was counting stars in the night sky.

Kilo approached as silent as a cat, and was now about five feet behind Kay Cee. Standing in the semi-darkness Kilo pulled the bandana down his face and let it rest around his neck. Kay Cee looked over his shoulder, and was startled half to death when he saw the shadowy figure standing in back of him. Once he realized that it was only Kilo he relaxed, and said, "Damn niggah, why in the hell you sneaking up on a niggah like that?"

Kay Cee took his eyes off of Kilo to zip up his pants. "Kilo, Gayle was just asking about you. She said…" When he turned around the chrome was shining in his face. He could see the glow from the street light beaming off the top of the gun.

"Kilo what the fuck!" he said devastated. Kilo just stared blankly from under his black New York Yankees fitted cap, showing no expressions of emotion. "Why you pulling out a gun on me? What part of the game is this?" Kay Cee cried out. His diamond chain was still glistering in the darkness.

After a moment of silence, Kilo spoke, "There was so many signs Kay Cee. I mean, you acting strange, coming home on an ankle bracelet for so long, and the whole ball till I fall bullshit! I should have known."

"You should have known what, fam'?"

"I'm not your fucking fam' niggah and I want you to die knowing that! Since we met Kay Cee I've looked out for you. I showed you how to be successful at the game you discovered. Everything I wanted out of life I wanted for you too. None of these niggahs from the Heights could get close to me son. When Omar put me on I trusted you, and I let you know everything," Kilo said softly as a tear dripped from both eyes. "How… could you spoil the legacy we had?"

"Kilo, man I don't know what to say. As far as I know I've kept it thorough ever since we were kids," Kay Cee said bitterly.

"Thorough! Niggah you call riding around with the fucking FEDs thorough, and then setting Reggie up with a fucking conspiracy case you dumb ass motherfuckah?" Kilo noticed Kay Cee's facial expressions change from worried to lifeless. "Yea, I know all about it Kay Cee. I even saw you with my own eyes. I never wanted to believe the shit, especially not about you."

"I admit that the FEDs have been harassing me lately. They were only showing me pictures and shit. You know how they do Kilo... I didn't have shit to do with Reggie and his peoples going down. How could you believe some bullshit rumors?"

"Kay Cee man, you know the game. I can't take any chances on you..."

"It's all lies!"

"My phones are tapped, my spots are getting raided just as fast as I open them, and you got caught with some fucking coke and a machine gun, and now your home flossing like shit is all good... Those are all facts niggah!" Kilo said while raising his voice, but quickly calmed back down.

"Kilo...man, I'm sorry. I'll do whatever you want for me to make it up," Kay Cee said as he started to sob. "It's two FBI agents. One name is Benny Thompson and the other is Mike Ledgeworth. They broke me down Kilo. They threatened me with five hundred months in federal prison if I didn't cooperate. In my mind I had no other choice... Fuck them crackers though man. We can still win this shit!" Kay Cee blurted out loudly.

Kilo shook his head as the truth played a song of relief. Everybody was right. Kay Cee was telling in order to avoid an asshole full of prison time. That in itself was bad, but what was even worse was the fact that he was willing to sacrifice Kilo's life in the process.

"Turn around you grimy, weak minded motherfuckah!" Kilo said sternly.

Obeying Kilo's instruction, Kay Cee slowly turned his back towards Kilo. At the same time he glanced over his left shoulder, and said, "You going to shoot me in my back son? This is how you want to end my story?"

Kilo aimed his weapon at the back of his head.

"Kay Cee you were in control of your own story. You chose to fold under the pressure of the white man. Nobody is to blame here but you. What goes around comes around...- I love you Kay Cee. Always have and always will," Kilo said slowly.

"Don't do it Kilo," Kay Cee cried. "I'll do the time. Just let me live, please!"

Silence controlled the night's air as Kilo held the gun outstretched. His gun began to lower.

"I'm about to have a baby," Kay Cee pleaded.

The gun rose. Kilo blinked his watery eyes, and then he pulled the trigger. (Boom, Boom, Boom!). Kay Cee's lifeless body slammed face first onto the hard cement. (Boom, Boom... Boom...Boom... Boom... Boom... Boom...Boom...Boom, Boom... Boom...Boom... Boom...Boom, Click!).

Kay Cee's body laid motionless after the bullets had mangled the back of his head and upper torso. Kilo emptied all seventeen shots into his best friend and now the adrenaline had him standing over the corpse pulling the trigger desperately for more shells to fire.

Realizing the bullets were gone, and his mission was complete Kilo pulled the bandana back up over his face. Instead of going back the way he came Kilo jumped a fence and disappeared into the darkness of a nearby alley. He never once looked back at what was left of Kay Cee's dead body...

CHAPTER SEVENTEEN
WHY??

"**A**lways pay your respects to the deceased. Life is short, and we each only have one life to live. No man wants to have an empty funeral when he passes away. Death is a time for mourning as well as a time for everyone to come together in remembrance of the dead. Even if the memories weren't that memorable for you..."

The very next morning after the shooting Kilo awoke just before the sun rose. Kiki was lying in bed next to him fast asleep. She was in the same position as when Kilo came home at 11:30 p.m. Kilo used her warm and soft body for comfort as his dreams brought horrible images to his head. He could vividly see the painful images of Kay Cee's body thumping violently against the concrete. The sound that his head made as it fell to the ground haunted him. The loud rhythm of the gun shots still banged in his head (Boom... Boom!). He stared at the ceiling of his dark bedroom and wiped away a forearm full of sweat.

Kilo leaned over and softly kissed Kiki on her neck. The perfume she wore smelled like fresh May flowers. He slowly ran his index finger along the baby hairs of her cheek, and then he eased his way out of the bed. What he had to do now was extremely important and even riskier than the actual homicide. Kilo was careful not to wake his sleeping beauty as he sat in the corner of the room in a small green rocking chair while pulling on his Polo jeans, and then his Timberland boots.

Kilo quietly went to the closet to grab his dark blue Polo snorkel jacket. His moves were calculated in order to make the least amount of noise. He definitely didn't need Kiki to wake up questioning him tonight, and easily being able to remember him leaving the house in the middle of the night; the morning after Kay Cee was murdered. He loved Kiki dearly, but in this situation no one was to be trusted.

Walking over the soft white carpet Kilo crept to the side of the bed where he slept. He carefully reached underneath the mattress, and then slowly pulled out the deadly nine millimeter that took his closest friends life. He quickly hid the gun behind his back and stood motionless as Kiki shifted into a more comfortable position. Once he was certain that she was still sleep, he then quietly made his was out of the peaceful suburban dwelling.

Riding through the deserted morning streets and highways Kilo made sure he wore his seat belt, obeyed all traffic signs, and cruised at the required speed limits of every area. He rode in total silence until he reached the inner city of downtown Rochester. As he rolled down Main Street a police cruiser was behind him obviously checking his license plates. Kilo avoided looking back through his rearview mirror as he waited at the red light. It was the longest light he ever stopped at. The only sounds in the car was his heart beating, and the signal light blinking as it lit up the arrow on the dashboard. When the light finally turned green after what seemed like an eternity, Kilo cautiously made his left hand turn. The police switched on his red lights and sirens as he sped off straight ahead. Kilo placed his right hand over his racing heart as he parked on a downtown side street between two huge office buildings.

Kilo exited Kiki's Benz and placed two quarters in the parking meter. He walked shortly down the quiet street, and then cut through a huge parking garage. It took him five minutes to make it to the opposite side. When he came out, he walked across the street and onto the sidewalk which would soon bring him to his destination. He had been here on three occasions before. The last time he was here was almost three years ago after murdering Raheem, and twice before that at the age of sixteen.

Kilo walked up to the railing and looked out across the waters. He pulled his gun from his coat pocket. He could see his every breath due to the cold morning temperature. He looked around to make sure that he was the only living soul around before he pressed a button on the side of the gun that was just above the rubber handle causing the empty clip to release into his left hand. Kilo held the long clip like a weird shaped rock, and then threw it out as far as he could. Then he held the barrow of the nine millimeter and flung it forward. Kilo watched as the shiny pistol was spinning around in the air before it splashed into the cold waters of the Genesee River.

—————«(0)»—————

Every pew was filled with mourning men, women, and children of all ages. All of whom was here to pay Kay Cee his final respects. His body lay inside of the baby blue casket peacefully and was surrounded with dozens of beautiful flowers.

Brothers who belonged to the church stood along the huge wall wearing black tuxedos. Kay Cee's mother Florence was seated in the very first row holding a white handkerchief under her nose as she sobbed at the untimely loss of her only son. Her youngest daughter, Ericka, sat next to her and was doing all she could to console her mother, plus shedding tears herself in remembrance of her brother Kenny. Tonya was there also. She was seated in the front row as well, crying her poor eyes out as Kiki did her best to comfort her. Tonya's belly held the life of the deceased man's son inside.

Kilo and Smooth C was in the third row of the church. Tears continuously flowed down Kilo's face. They were true tears of pain and regret as he watched from behind, as Kiki wiped Tonya's face with a napkin.

There was a big picture of Kay Cee on top of the bottom half of his casket. In the photo Kay Cee had a huge smile on his face that seemed to be directed at Kilo. Kay Cee's eyes seemed to be staring directly at his killer through the crowd of people.

"No matter how we felt about Kay Cee, we got to kill the niggah responsible for this Kilo," Smooth C whispered in his ear.

This was the first time during the week Kay Cee had been dead that Kilo really felt any guilt. All along he'd been trying to convince himself that he did the right thing. He refused to think of the pain he caused Kay Cee's family. He knew from growing up around Ms. Conway that she loved her only son dearly. She was always there when Kay Cee was in trouble, and sometimes she even saved Kilo's ass too. Kilo disregarded the fact that Kay Cee was about to have a child. Despite it all he still savagely laid someone whom he referred to as "a brother from another mother" to rest all in the name of the streets.

"In due time Smooth C the truth will come to the light. It's the way of the world," Kilo responded as the choir began a song that brought Tonya to her feet in tears. Almost half of the church stood and sung along.

Kilo looked around at all of the people he had hurt. He was the reason that the choir was singing those sad songs, and he was responsible for the crying faces. His actions had affected so many innocent lives, but what hurt him the most was seeing Tonya, pregnant. She looked so mature today and in search of answers. She needed closure to the mystery of who stole her son's father away from them. Kilo's pride had superseded the love he had for Kay Cee, and the respect he had for the Conway family. None of Kay Cee's family spoke to him which added to the fact that he really had no business attending.

The choir's angelic voices faded, and the reverend slowly made his way to the podium. "Brother and sisters we are unfortunately gathered in the house of the Lord to put to rest a wonderful young man. Kenny Conway was physically taken away from us, but in spirit he will always warm the hearts of his loved ones. Praise God! He is survived by his mother Ms. Florence Conway and three lovely sisters: Malinda, Felicia, and Ericka Conway... Kenny was also expecting a child with his girlfriend Tonya Jones in two months. I ask that we all keep her in our prayers as she guides this child," said the Rev. Earl T. Poke.

After a couple more tear compelling songs from the choir, Kay Cee's mother was invited up to say a few words on her son's behalf. She took her time as she approached the podium. She was brown complexioned, grey haired, and she had a pleasant appearance. Softly she said, "I... am the mother of Kenny. My baby was brutally murdered. He was stolen away from us for no apparent reason. My loss... will take me years to overcome- if ever. Kenny was a smart and very sweet young man. He was expecting his first child in only a few months... Tymer! Why? Why did you kill my son?" Florence yelled at Kilo. "They told me you did this!!!"

There was a "gasp!" in the congregation as all eyes shifted to Kilo. The reverend and a few church elders struggled to take Ms. Conway to the back office of the church. She could be heard hysterically yelling down the hallway, "Why? He killed me baby!!!"

Kilo was more surprised at her outburst as anyone else as he aimlessly stared back into the shocked faces of the church.

Tonya pushed Kiki's arm from around her shoulders, and then jumped up heading for Kilo in a sudden rage. Kiki quickly grabbed a hand full of Tonya's hair from behind and viciously dragged her down to the floor. She totally disregarded the fact that Tonya was pregnant. Erica and her two sisters ran over and started punching and kicking Kiki while she was on top of Tonya. Smooth C immediately jumped over the three pews separating him from the brawl and punched Erica in her face sending her to the floor unconscious.

The male ushers and brothers ran over to break up the fight that had shamefully erupted in the house of the Lord. Punches were still being thrown as Kilo joined the myriad of people hurrying out the front door.

Kilo pulled up in front of the church in minutes driving Kiki's Benz. After a while Smooth C and Kiki came storming out of the church. The crowd that stood outside lowered their heads in disgust as they brushed by. Once the two were inside of the car, Kilo wasted no time speeding away from the curb.

"Those bitches must be crazy!" Kiki yelled. Her hair was now made into a mess and her beautiful black Gucci dress was tore from the shoulder strap down to its waist. The bra she had on was the only shield to her left breast being exposed. She pulled down her visor and examined the small scratches on her pretty face in the mirror. "Kilo, why in the fuck would Flo' think you killed her son? I swear to God you better not of had shit to do with that!"

"You know I didn't kill that niggah! The hoods been saying that bullshit, but that was my fucking man in that casket!" Kilo tried to explain, while Kiki was crying waterfalls into her palms.

It was a rumor going around that Kilo killed Kay Cee over some unpaid money. It only escalated when Kilo failed to show any real emotion after his right hand man was found dead in back of a store, riddled with bullets. Once Kilo heard the rumor he called Flo' and told her, "Ms. Conway I'm sorry about what happened to Kenny. And there's something I want to clear up before it gets back to you… There are some who think I had a part in Kenny's murder, but I want to tell you personally that their wrong. I would never, ever do anything like this to Kenny. I loved him like a brother." Her response was that she wouldn't listen to any of the rumors until she knew more. Kilo was confused as to why she would point him out to the entire church as her son's killer so soon after their conversation.

"I knocked one of those whores the fuck out," Smooth C yelled from the back seat. "I break bitches jaws too when it comes to my sister!"

"Kiki look at me," Kilo begged. "I didn't have anything to do with it. I promise."

"I can't keep going through this shit anymore...You haven't

changed Kilo. Take me to my mother's house. I never want to see you again. You claim to be a major niggah, but to me you're nothing more than a fucking serial killer!" Kiki said.

Without thinking, Kilo back slapped Kiki so hard that her head slammed up against the passenger's window. She held the side of her stinging face as she succumbed to more shock than pain.

Smooth C lunged up from the back seat, and grabbed Kilo tightly by the neck with his right hand, and said dangerously, "Niggah if you ever hit my sister again I'll fuck you up!" He then wisely released his grip.

"I hate you Kilo!" Kiki screamed.

Her words penetrated through his heart with the force of a bullet. Kilo stepped on the clutch and violently shook the stick from side to side. "Fuck you then bitch! And Smooth C niggah you got that one, but never again will you get away with touching me motherfuckah."

"Whatever! You heard what the fuck I said, son."

Kilo jumped out of the car and slammed the door as hard as he possibly could. He casually walked away from the scene as angry drivers blew their horns at the black Benz until Kiki slid over to the driver's position, slammed the stick in first gear, and then sped away from the intersection.

CHAPTER EIGHTEEN
BREAK UP TO MAKE UP

"**Sometimes the bad situations are needed to truly bring people closer together. In all relationships there will be some type of differences. A wise man will give the other their 'space and time' apart until the right time to attempt peace again. But if there is no chance of reconciliation, part ways and learn from your mistakes...**"

Empty bags and sandwich wrappers from McDonalds and Wendy's were scattered all over the living room table and the kitchen counter. The usual smell of wonderful potpourri was now just a mere aroma of old weed smoke. The huge Webster house hadn't been a home since Kiki left. It was so dirty; to call it a pig sty would be a compliment.

For the first time since the three bedroom and two bathroom home was built had another woman been there to enjoy its coziness other than Keisha. This was the ultimate disrespect for Kiki that Kilo had ever shown. It wasn't necessarily done to get even, but the loneliness he felt without Kiki made him yearn for the special comfort of a woman.

Sidney, an exotic Australian model was the last of three women Kilo had invited to his home to temporarily replace Kiki. She was five feet- eleven inches tall and thick as hell. She was a part of the phenomenon of white women with big asses. Her long blond hair hung down into a curly ponytail. She was a beautiful and sexy female.

It was Sidney's distinct accent that seduced Kilo when he first met her at the Jewelry Store. She was talking to a salesmen about a ring she was getting appraised.

The Italian salesmen said, "I'm sorry, but it's only a fifty dollar cubic zirconium. The only thing that's real is the fourteen karat gold."

She said, "It can't be a fake. He said that he loved me! How could he do this to me?"

She was vulnerable to Kilo's game as he slid up next to her at the perfect time, and whispered, "He doesn't understand the value of your woman's worth, so how could you expect him to buy you something equally expensive? My name is Kilo. Call me later and I'm guaranteed to take your mind off of the loser!"

Sidney poked her breast implants out, and then enhanced her accent, "I can't wait until later. I need to feel wanted now!"

The salesmen smiled, and gave Kilo the thumbs up as they walked out of the door.

For the last two days now Sidney had been in Webster with Kilo performing any sexual favor he requested. She didn't want to leave. Kilo had sexed her so good in all kinds of different positions that when he walked her to the door tears ran down her face leaving a mascara stream. She said, "Kilo it's been nice meeting you. Your so gangster and you can fuck so well. If things don't work out with Keisha, call me?"- Then she dropped down to her knees and sucked his erection in a heat of passion before Kilo sent her home to deal with her cheap ass fiancé.

After Sidney departed Kilo decided that today enough was enough. The King needed his Queen back to tend to his needs, and her castle. He braced himself for resistance as the phone to Kiki's mother's house rung. "Hello," a female's voice answered warmly.

"Hi... Diane. Is Keisha there?" Kilo asked shyly.

"Tymer you know I'm mad at you," Diane said. "Since when did you start hitting on women? You know that a real man is not supposed to hurt the ones he love. Or else who would stand by your side when you really need them?"

"Miss Jackson I'm so sorry. I never hit Keisha before and I shouldn't have had then either, and for the last couple of days I've been feeling the pain of not having her," Kilo said sincerely.

"Well baby you and I both know that Keisha has been by your side strong for all of these years. Now is not the time to begin treating her other than anything but the black queen she was born to be. Plus all women deserve that same respect Kilo... Now I've heard rumors about what happened last week, and I don't expect for you to talk openly to me about it, but the Lord knows I hope what I've heard isn't true," Diane said in reference to the Kay Cee situation.

"If you're talking about what I think, then of course not. And Keisha of all people should know that," Kilo responded.

"Tymer you stay out of trouble, you hear. You don't want too many people to be praying on your downfall because prayer gets stronger with numbers. Keep your nose clean, and I'll continue to pray for you as I have been for the longest, okay?"

"Yes Diane. I will."

Kilo heard Diane scream into the house for Kiki. When she came to the phone, she asked her mom who was on the line, and then she yelled at Kilo, "What?"

"Kiki what's up?" Kilo asked.

"I'm okay, but to be honest I was better before you called."

"Come on girl, don't treat me like that. I miss you to death over here. Life isn't the same without your smell, your laughter, or even your shit talking," Kilo said hoping she'll laugh.

"I thought by now you'll be on America's Most Wanted... Either you don't understand or you just don't care about all of the shit you put me through. Why is it that every time a niggah has a good girl, someone who really cares for his ass, he finds a way to fuck shit up?" Kiki asked.

"Listen Kiki, I talked to Flo' again yesterday and we straightened everything out. She was listening to them cowards in the hood. She didn't really believe I had anything to do with her son's death anyways... I need you to come back home. Please Kiki?" Kilo begged.

She said, "I'm scared Kilo. You fucking hit me in front of my brother- after I got jumped at a funeral for your ass! I'll be dumb if I come back."

"So what are you going to do now, find another niggah after all that we've been through?" Kilo asked.

"I don't know what I want to do, but the last thing on my mind is another niggah Kilo. It'll take me years to find someone who will treat me how you do," she admitted.

"What do I have to do for you to come back Keisha?" Kilo asked. He knew that she liked being called her real name.

"The only way I can come back home Kilo is if you get out of those damn streets. I worry about your safety when you're out there. Marketview Heights is getting more and more dangerous every day. Just look at what happened to Kay Cee. We grew up with that boy and now he's dead. When will you learn Kilo?" Kiki asked.

"Nothing good comes overnight," Kilo whispered. "But I can promise that soon we'll be able to leave Rochester. I promise. Now will you come home and warm up this house with your love?"

Kiki sat on the couch in her mother's living room wearing a pair of white pajamas with red heart decorations. She slowly took her thumb out of her mouth, and then with the same hand she used it to rub her pregnant stomach. She had been waiting by the phone for Kilo's call for days. She loved Kilo and would die for him in a single heartbeat.

"I'm on my way boy!" she said with a precious smile.

⋙⠿⋘

The excited club squeezed and pushed to the front of S & T's nightclub. It was extremely packed as usual on Sunday's. The women made up the majority of the crowd as they outnumbered the men by a ratio of seven to one.

Ten curvaceous women filled the stage, and began wildly shaking their asses to the beats of the Reggae music that was rocking the club. The lights were dim, and the atmosphere was filled with weed smoke. The beautiful women were competing for one thousand dollars in the monthly 'Back That Ass Up' contest. Their outfits were sexy and many gave strippers a run for their money.

Kilo stood in front of the stage holding a bottle of Ciroc. He was surrounded by a group of young hustlers from Marketview Heights. They stood around Kilo intently observing the club for potential threats the way bodyguards would.

Kilo was drunk and fantasizing about fucking the short light-skinned female who was on stage dancing in the middle of the other women. She was standing with her back facing the crowd as she placed her hands on the sides of her waist, and then began to make her forty-five inch ass cheeks bounce rapidly up and down. The sexy dancer caught Kilo watching her and was now putting on a show specifically for him. She fell down to the floor in a split and made her ass lift up and down as her pussy banged onto the stage. Kilo licked his lips, pulled on his blunt, and sipped from the bottle with his free hand.

Kilo walked over to the wall and stood alone. He noticed that Steal kept watching him from across the dance floor. When Kilo attempted to say, "What's up?" with a head motion, Steal ignored him and returned a facial expression that read, "Fuck you niggah!" For the rest of the night Kilo didn't pay Steal much more attention as he continued to party.

Kilo had a good feeling that he was under investigation for the murder of Kay Cee. Somebody was destined to have had mentioned his name to the police, especially after Kay Cee's mother yelled out his name at the funeral. It was now only a matter of time before they would drag him downtown for questioning. His plan was to flee from Rochester in a few weeks, and never return again. It would look too suspicious if he'd leave now so suddenly. So just in case he got arrested and dragged to jail in handcuffs before he could leave town, Kilo was determined to party until it was all over.

The ten beautiful ladies lined across the stage for the announcement of the contest winner. The dancer who Kilo lusted for was marked by a red ribbon attached to her bra as number seven. She was about five feet tall and wore a short hair style like Jada Pinkett-Smith. Her thighs were thick and the gap between her legs left her pussy sitting out in the open. Kilo wanted her so bad.

Kilo looked around again for Steal, but couldn't spot him nowhere as the crowd stood still in anticipation. He wanted to keep an eye on Steal just in case the look he gave meant beef. If Steal was to try something tonight Kilo was prepared to kill him right in the club. He wouldn't give him a chance to cry that, "I was drunk last night," bullshit. Nope, he'd have to explain that to his maker if he fucked with Kilo anytime soon.

After Kay Cee's funeral Kilo stopped dealing with reason. Smooth C was still acting like a bitch, and without admitting it Kilo was feeling alone in the streets minus his other half, Kay Cee. Basically he was feeling like the world was against him. Not only was he always prepared to draw the first blood, but he also vowed to kill anyone who crossed him again.

Excited after winning, dancer #7 walked off the stage and headed straight for Kilo. He didn't notice her approaching until she began tugging on the sleeve of his shirt. "Hi sexy! Did you see anything you liked?" she asked as she rose to her tippy toes to whisper in his ear.

"Of course I did. I liked the way you made your ass cheeks clap. And that split you did was crazy," Kilo said looking her short body up and down. "Hopefully I can be the judge to determine whether or not you really have the best ass?"

"How would you be able to tell without fucking any of the other contestants?" she asked.

"Good question. Maybe I can just judge your pussy personally.

Believe me; I know good pussy when I get it."

"Well to be honest I have to get back home to my man before the niggah gets suicidal and shit, but you can take my number and maybe fuck me another time?" she suggested.

"I can do that, but I was hoping to get some of that tonight. I mean excuse me for being impatient, but I know good pussy when I see it too!" he whispered.

She smiled at Kilo's straightforwardness. She dug into her handbag to retrieve her cell phone. She entered Kilo's number and saved it. The sexy dancer pulled Kilo by the arm and led him into a dark corner on the side of the stage. There was a huge burgundy curtain that provided them privacy.

She said, "I can't give you any pussy tonight because I know my man will want to fuck me when I get home, but I do want to suck your dick though... I know I'm the best at that!"

The beautiful dancer dropped down to her knees and quickly found Kilo's erection and guided it into her mouth. She went to work as she was destined to keep her crown. Kilo peeped around the curtain to make sure the ghost was clear. He didn't want any of his old females to spot him getting his dick sucked in the club, and use that as an excuse not to leave with him once it was over.

The weed and alcohol together made him feel like he was floating on cloud nine. He was getting great slow head from a beautiful woman whom he didn't even catch her name. She made love to his dick with her tongue until Kilo busted a nut in her small mouth and partially over her pretty face as he pulled away.

"Excuse me for that... my fault. I can only imagine what your pussy is like," Kilo said while fixing his pants.

While wiping his cream from her face, she said, "It's cool... What's your name?"

"Kilo."

"I'm Beauty. I've heard about you before. All of the ladies love you. My home girls are going to think I'm lying when I tell them you came on my face," she said laughing. "...Kilo I usually charge niggahs a hundred dollars for sucking dick, but being that I just won a grand by dancing for you, I'll catch you next time." Beauty then straightened her clothes and left Kilo behind the curtain.

For the rest of the night Kilo continued to enjoy himself as if he didn't have a worry in the world. The way things were going he didn't really know if he was celebrating the beginning or the ending of his young life. *'Fuck it,'* Kilo thought. *'At least a niggah still alive to celebrate.'*

CHAPTER NINETEEN
SNEAK ATTACK PT. 1

"**W**hen things start to go wrong many times it only gets worse before getting better. Some things in life a person just can't plan for. Your emotional response to these circumstances is the only way to make it a little easier to deal with..."

Once Smooth C spotted his sister's Benz parked out front, he decided not to go inside of the club. He knew that it was Kilo driving because Kiki would never allow herself to be caught dead in a hood club like S & T's. It was in her mind 'slut central'. Kiki only partied at main events like concerts, stage plays, and comedy shows.

Kiki had forgiven Kilo for slapping the shit out of her a few weeks ago, but Smooth C still held animosity against him for disrespecting his sister in front of him. He felt the slap himself that rocked his sister's head. Ever since that day he didn't speak to Kilo and avoided being in the same place with him for too long. Kilo hitting Kiki was a violation deserving of gun play. Kay Cee's funeral was the only reason Smooth C didn't bring his gun, which ultimately saved Kilo from getting shot.

Smooth C slowly cruised through the crowded parking lot in back of the club. It seemed to be more excitement outside than it was inside. This was how it was every weekend at S & T's despite the cold November weather.

Being that he was with a young lady himself; Smooth C was kind of mad that he couldn't talk to any of the half-drunk and horny women that ran back and forth to the different sets of niggahs who were in the parking lot, pimping.

Some brothers had their music blasting from open trunks, while others played DVD's on thirty inch screens to be viewed by the female by passers. Fancy foreign cars and big luxury SUV's were parked all throughout the huge parking lot. Niggahs stood outside of their vehicles in crowds, passing blunts around in a cipher. They were dressed to impress. Many had on expensive fur coats and big platinum chains hanging from their necks.

This was all done in a natural competition to show which hustler was getting the most money. Every niggah knew that the more you seemed to be shining the more women heads would turn in your direction, and at the end of the day the money and drugs wouldn't be shit without any pussy. Niggahs came to S & T's trying to leave with a nocturnal freak, and it was a fact that they only flocked to major niggahs who looked like major figures.

The majority of the crowd was from Marketview Heights. Smooth C intended on bringing Foxy to S & T's for a few drinks to celebrate her eighteenth birthday, and then take her to a hotel. Since Kilo was inside; riding through the lot and maybe parking for a minute would have to do.

Smooth C lowered the Plies music, and said, "Foxy I was going to take you inside, but I see that my sister's boyfriend, Kilo, is in there tonight and I'm not really fucking with him right now. So maybe next week we could come back, alright?"

"Fine, that's cool with me. I'm just chilling over here," she said as she relaxed on the cream, butter soft leather passenger's seat. Her hair hung down and hid most of her chocolate face. Smooth C was feeling Foxy's style and could tell that she had been through a lot during her short amount of time living. Tonight was the first time they really had a chance to chill and Smooth C wanted to get to know her more. She was a little different than the females his age that lived in the Heights.

"Foxy, I'm really feeling you're laid back style," Smooth C said as he carefully maneuvered around the drunken pedestrians. "Hopefully you can recognize a real niggah when you see one, and try to be real with me."

She said, "I know you're official Smooth C. You are the coolest niggah I ever met, but the question is can you be real with me?"

"I only know real. I'm just looking for a female who could always hold me down, play her position, and be willing to do something positive with herself."

"That's not hard for me. You'll just have to show me how to do the things you like and teach me not to do shit you dislike," she said.

Smooth C smiled, and said, "I can do that sexy."

Foxy met Smooth C at the Main Street Armory last week when Young Jeezy came to Rochester to do a concert. She was glad to meet Smooth C and felt lucky to wind up in the midst of a real niggah from Marketview Heights. Smooth C was one of the genuine ones unlike the character, Steal, whom she met before. Foxy knew that Smooth C's young ass was paid and for that reason alone she'd do anything for him upon request. She loved hustlers, especially the ones who were her age and getting real money.

Foxy took a deep pull from the mint green weed she was smoking, and passed the canoed blunt back to her man.

Smooth C looked at the awkward burning blunt, and said, "See this is something I don't like." He showed her the blunt so she'd know what he was talking about. "This happens when you pull on it too hard. It causes one side to burn faster than the other. But don't worry it can be fixed."

"I'm sorry," Foxy said with a smile. She took one last look around the parking lot full of hustlers and partying women before Smooth C turned right onto North Street.

As Smooth C sped to the nearest hotel in his brand new BMW, Foxy unzipped his pants and started sucking on his dick as he drove.

"Man! Now that's some shit I do like," Smooth C cooed as Plies screamed through the speakers, "I can make your everyday, like a big time model!"

—=≡»«(●)»«≡=—

The threesome was on their way back from the movie theater. They went to watch a new scary movie where a little girl possessed some type of power which enabled her to kill with only a deep thought. Kiki, Renee, and their other close friend Tasha screamed throughout the entire movie. In one scene the demon-possessed girl made a Chinese sword glide across the room and chop off an old lady's head. The girls screamed to the top of their lungs for a full five minutes until a love scene cooled them down.

Kiki could still vision the blood, the cries for help, and all of the eerie music of the horror film. On the way home she called Kilo's cell phone about ten times, but received no answer. It was still early and she figured that he didn't want to answer his phone in the midst of a crowded club. It was 1:30 a.m. and she wanted to make sure Kilo would come straight home after the club let out, but knowing him he'd probably run around the city for about two extra hours doing nothing. Besides being horny, she needed the security of a man after watching that scary ass movie.

Renee chose to drop Kiki off in Webster first so she could have Tasha to ride back with her into the city; plus they only lived a few blocks away from one another in the peaceful neighborhood of Cornhill.

As they rode to the suburbs the three close friends laughed and joked like they were still freshmen at Monroe High School. But today the jokes were more adult oriented, and sometimes X-rated.

"I hope I still have batteries at home for my dildo," Tasha said. She was the freak out of the crew. Renee and Kiki both were in relationships and only cheated when they indulged in one of Tasha's extremely graphic narrations of her promiscuous sex life. "I would call Tyrone, but his dick is not eighteen inches, and I know for a fact he can't last all night like my dildo could!"

"Damn, why in the hell did Terrance have to go to Atlanta for his mother's funeral?" Renee asked and was really expecting an answer.

"Bitch you know you not right for that. He's putting his mother to rest and all you can do is think about dick. You should be ashamed of yourself!" Tasha interrupted.

"Hell yes! That niggah has nine inches and he lasts all night... I miss Baby Daddy. He could of waited until he passed away to see her ass for all I care."

"Renee God is going to fuck you up one day because you play with the wrong shit. You a crazy bitch! That's why Terrance didn't take your ass with him to Atlanta," Tasha yelled.

"For your information, I decided to stay home. You get a man and a real dick before you start talking, bitch," Renee said while reaching one hand back for a five from Kiki.

"Well luckily for me, my man is going to come home tonight and tear it up... But I don't know why Kilo is not texting me or answering my calls. He knows it's me," Kiki said as she dialed Kilo's number again and got no answer. "Fuck! He does this shit every weekend."

Renee finally pulled into Kiki's driveway and parked as close to the two car garage as possible. All of the lights were off in the home and Kiki just knew she would be lonely until Kilo arrived.

"You two should come in until Kilo gets here?" Kiki asked.

Renee and Tasha both said in unison, "Hell no."

"Well fuck you then. I didn't want you greedy hoes to come in anyways," Kiki snapped as she opened the back door of Renee's cherry red Acura Integra.

"You better make sure Kilo takes it easy on that pregnant pussy. You know niggahs love that knocked-up wet wet. He going to be drilling your ass like he in Iraq looking for oil," Renee advised with much laughter.

"Bitch please," Kiki said simply.

Tasha rolled down the passenger's window, and asked, "Keisha, you didn't tell Kilo you were pregnant yet, huh?"

"No. But I will tell him soon. I just don't know how he will react," Kiki replied while standing in the driveway.

"Well he needs to know Keisha. He will be happy. Any niggah would love to have a family with you girl," Tasha said realizing that Kiki was the exact opposite of herself.

"Tasha, will you let that damn girl go so I can take my ass to sleep. She knows she has to tell that man sooner or later," Renee pleaded.

"Bye ladies. I will call tomorrow. Love you," Kiki said as she proceeded to her front door.

Renee waited in the driveway until Kiki opened the front door and turned on the hallway lights. Kiki waived goodbye from the doorway. Renee backed out of the driveway and hit the horn three quick times before speeding down Kiki's small, quiet street.

Kiki closed the door, and then kicked off her white and pink Nike's onto a rug that read: *Kilo and Keisha's Castle*. She started to punch in the security code to the alarm system when she realized that it was never set. Not setting the alarm had become a habit for the couple. Being surrounded by well off middle-class white people made it easy to forget to set the alarm sometimes. In the suburb of Webster it was even okay to occasionally leave the front door wide open from time to time.

Kiki walked over to the house phone and dialed Kilo's number again. Still there was no answer. 'Damn!' she thought.

She figured that if she went upstairs to take a shower Kilo would be home by the time she finished. Kiki was mad as hell that he was not answering her calls, but from past experiences similar to now Kilo would come home from the club drunk and fuck her into two or three rough orgasms. He was always at his sexual best when alcohol was in his system.

With that thought in mind wetness began to moisten her panties. Kiki began to lazily jog up the steps. When she turned right to begin the next set of stairs, she was frightened almost to death. A big black figure lunged at her from behind the wall that divided the two sets of stairs. Kiki managed to exhale a loud piercing scream before the huge man grabbed her by the neck and slammed her against the wall. The impact caused two paintings to crash to the floor. The man forcefully covered her mouth with his huge left hand.

Kiki kicked and scratched at her attacker's hand until she was stunned by the sight of a second man descending from the darkness of the staircase brandishing a chrome handgun. She could tell that the red beam was aimed directly at her forehead. Kiki ceased the struggle and was now ready to negotiate.

"Bitch if you want to live, you will calm the fuck down! All you have to do is the right thing. But if you chose not to I promise you will die tonight," Steal warned from behind a black ski mask.

Black stepped up and touched his gun to the side of Kiki's temple. He was also wearing a ski mask and they both were equipped with black hoods and leather gloves.

"I'm about to let go of your mouth and you better not start screaming again, okay?" Steal asked as he grabbed a hand full of Kiki's hair. With a simple head motion she agreed to be quiet.

Steal led Kiki back down the steps by her hair and once in the living room he pushed her onto the couch. All she could do was curse Kilo out in her head. *'Where in the fuck are you Kilo? Why did you have to go to the club tonight? I should have never taken your ass back!'* She silently thanked God that Renee and Tasha did not come inside. She would hate for them to be hurt for something she knew involved Kilo.

"You know what we want. Just tell us where your faggot ass boyfriend Kilo keeps his money, and then we'll leave," Steal demanded.

From the very first day Kilo started hustling he would always advise Kiki about the ills of his lifestyle. He knew that one day there will be somebody with the balls to try and rob him. Most of his street life he tried to conceal from Kiki, but he always tried to teach her what to do in case of a robbery. But all of his scenarios involved them both at gunpoint. Kilo once advised, "Let me do all of the talking. Don't scream or act too scared. I will handle it."

That was easy for Kilo to say, but how could she not be scared while alone, pregnant, and threatened by two niggahs who she can't even see their faces? Kilo also once told her, "If the stickup kids are wearing masks, then they more than likely did not come to kill. It's the ones who are robbing you without masks that you better comply with quickly. They plan to kill anyways so don't give them extra reasons to pull their triggers."

The one thing that Kilo reiterated over and over again was, "Never ever try to save the money! Why risk getting killed to protect something you can have again tomorrow? Fuck the money!" Kiki remembered.

Black never took the gun or his lustful eyes off of Kiki as she sat quietly in fear. She was gorgeous. He had been watching her all night at the movies as she sat in the front row with her friends, screaming to the top of their lungs like kids. He was turned on by the way Kiki carried herself, smiled, and stood with the arch in her lower back. Black fanaticized about fucking her and taking her back to Buffalo with him and saying fuck Steal. He had never been with a female who was even close to how pretty Kiki was.

Tonight Steal's plan for revenge was underway. He had followed Kilo to the club while ordering Black to stay close to Kiki. Black was inside of the dark movie theater when his cell phone rung. He stepped out of the theater, and answered Steal's call, "Black. The time is now. Kilo is at club S & T's dead as drunk. Moet has him wrapped up. Leave that bitch there and meet me in Webster at the niggah house!" This conversation was just the beginning of the plan.

"Kilo doesn't keep money here. If he did I would not know where he hides it. He doesn't trust anyone...not even me," Kiki said as she continuously sobbed.

Black stepped closer, and then slapped the shit out of Kiki causing her to fall sideways onto the couch.

"Chill the fuck out!" Steal screamed at Black, and then he said nicely to Kiki, "Shorty, don't play no games with me. This shit is life or death for you right now. That niggah Kilo is probably somewhere fucking another female while you possibly breathing your last breaths. So, I will ask you again. Where is the money?"

All Kiki kept thinking about was the young life living inside of her. The one Kilo did not even know existed. She knew that it would be disastrous for her to continue taking this physical and mental abuse. "I'm pregnant! I'm fucking pregnant..." she cried.

Black smiled at her outburst. It was a great sign of weakness which if exploited could get her to talk and if not it would be the perfect place to send a bullet. Black stuck the nose of his chrome .45 caliber handgun to the side of Kiki's stomach, which was partially exposed while lying on her side. He said, "Well baby girl you can't keep bullshitting us then, huh? Just come clean with the stash and we'll leave your pregnant ass alone, or I will have to shoot you for the wasted time."

Black looked down and noticed Kiki was wearing a pair of yellow panties. He could feel himself growing in his pants.

"I am going to count to five and then I want answers. If not I'm going to leave you two alone. After he takes some of that pregnant pussy, I am sure he will body your ass too. So it's up to you for real. We finished playing around!" Steal said sternly.

Black smiled at Steal's threat. He loved the idea of being able to fuck Kiki. He grabbed a hand full of her breast, while he tightly pressed his gun into her side with his other hand. Black leaned forward and licked her neck and began sucking on her ear.

Kiki shouted, "Okay, get the fuck off of me you rapist! He stashes his money at his uncle's house... Every fucking dime! I'll take you there."

Steal looked at Black, and said, "Back up niggah. Let her take us to his uncle's house. I believe her ass for some reason."

Kiki sat up on the couch and buried her head into her palms.

"You are lucky. I was about to fuck the shit out of you girl!" Black said while holding onto his hard on through his pants...

CHAPTER TWENTY
SNEAK ATTACK PT. 2

"The thing that makes life so difficult is the fact that it is so unpredictable. It's hard to accept responsibility for one's own actions when it is the people around you who are suffering the most. Life is a game and it never ever plays fair..."

Kilo stumbled out of S & T's with his arm wrapped around Moet's slim shoulders. He was pissy drunk from so much alcohol consumption. It had been a long time since he was able to really enjoy himself at a Rochester club without there being any fights or arguments. Tonight Kilo was able to drink, flirt, and smoke weed without any interruptions up until the last farewell song was played.

Kilo was feeling good and did not have a care in the world. He even forgot about the way Steal was acting as the night passed. Kilo made a mental note to confront Steal the next time he seen him just to make sure there was not any hard feelings. Kilo always made it his business to step to potential beef before a niggah could muster the heart to attack him first. In this game; the offense usually wins.

Kilo opened the passenger's door to Kiki's Benz and slapped Moet on her round ass as she carefully slid inside. Kilo made his way to the driver's side. While still standing in the street, he yelled, "Fuck the world!"

The heavy crowd who were still standing around began to scream, "Marketview Heights!" and repeated, "Fuck the world!"

Every hustler young or old in some way wanted to be just like Kilo. They all admired his street smarts, his style, and the power Kilo had over the hood. He was the definition of a true hustler and was well respected in Marketview Heights. Whenever a hustler beat a murder charge, and then came home to allegedly put seventeen shots into their best friend- it would be a challenge to question that man's street credibility.

Many truly loved Kilo, but there were a lot of others who secretly hated him for being so successful. It's a good thing that the two emotions equaled out to respect and that was all that mattered.

Kilo could feel the energy he created. He understood that the streets were watching him for any signs of weakness and in order for him to stay on top he always had to maintain a certain disposition at all times. For him Kiki was his only weakness. She was the person who if harmed, he would kill and risk destroying everything in his path. She had been there through the good, the bad, and the indifferent. Knowing that she was well taken care of was the main reason he could roam the streets and hustle with such confidence. He knew that his backbone would always be there.

Before Kilo pulled away, he entered the numbers to his house into his cell phone. While the phone was ringing he put his index finger in front of his lips warning Moet to be quiet. There was no answer. Kilo hung up when the call went to voice message. He didn't want to call her cell phone while she was with her nosey as friends.

Kilo put fire to the end of a long blunt that was filled with exotic weed. "Moet, I have to be home in a couple hours but until then we can do whatever. Where you want to go?" Kilo asked.

Moet was an older woman from the west side's notorious Thurston Avenue. She was thick, beautiful, and had more game than the rapper from Compton. Moet approached Kilo a few weeks ago for a short introduction, but they had yet to chill since. Tonight Moet did everything in her power to make sure Kilo went home with her. All night she danced over his hard on, licked his neck, and frequently guided his hand between her moist legs. She was not taking no for an answer.

"Kilo my pussy is so wet. I need for you to sex me into an orgasm... Can you do that for me young buck?" Moet leaned over and whispered into Kilo's ear.

Moet's pretty brown complexion, natural long hair, and extremely round ass had tempted the most faithful men to cheat and spend their money on her. Tonight she was being extra persistent with Kilo because she was promised a thousand dollars by her ex-husband, Steal, if she was able to keep Kilo occupied for a few hours after the club. "Let's ride out to Charlotte Beach, so we could fuck on the pier!" Moet added.

"Okay, that sounds like a plan," Kilo said with a smile as he pulled away from S & T's.

⸺ ◉ ⸺

Kiki rode back into the city in unimaginable fear after being abducted from her peaceful home. From the back seat, Black held his gun to her ribs while she sat nervously in the passenger's seat. Kiki had no idea how tonight would play out, but she prayed Freddie or Lisa would not be harmed by her attackers.

Steal drove in complete silence with his eyes glued to the road. He was on a mission. For him times were rough in the streets since coming home after a parole violation. Hunger was the underlying factor for his current robbery sprees. The dark tinted windows of the 300c allowed Black and Steal to ride with the masks still covering their faces.

During the ride, Kiki prayed that the cops would pull them over, but the truth was that they were now parked down the street from Freddie's home.

The white two-story house looked so quiet and peaceful. If Kiki was not following Kilo's vague instructions, she would have never told them where the money was stashed. *'Never try to protect the money!'* Kilo whispered again in her ear.

For some reason Kiki felt like she would one day regret this risky decision. But all she really wanted was for them to take the money and leave without harming anyone just as they had promised back at the house.

With both hands Kiki rubbed the sides of her stomach. She was trying her best to remain calm for the baby's sake. Her face was still throbbing from where Black had slapped her hard enough to break the skin on her left cheek. And even though it was not bleeding- it stung every time tears flowed through the small cut.

Steal held a small .38 to the side of Kiki's head as they sat in wait. He was contemplating on how to proceed. The music was playing real low and the voice of Max B filled the car.

"Don't worry baby girl. In a few minutes all of this shit will be just a bad memory. But you know memories don't live like people do. Especially strong people," Steal told Kiki from under his black mask.

Steal had never planned on hurting Kiki. He watched her grow up in Marketview Heights before he went to prison. Besides he had a wife and daughter of his own. So if he could get his hands on the money without actually having to harm her, everything would be fine. It was just unfortunate that he needed to use her to get to the cash. It was a part of the game which everyone knew doesn't play fair. Sometimes important rules had to be broken.

"Black, go knock on the door to see if they will open. And once they do, force your way inside. Tie they asses up and we coming in right behind you," Steal ordered. "If they don't open just kick the fucking door down."

As commanded, Black stuffed his gun inside his waist and exited the car. While on the side of the car he removed his mask and quickly pulled the hood over his head before Kiki could see him.

"What if he shoots the old man and his wife?" Kiki asked, as they watched Black walking up the sidewalk towards Freddie's house. Black was now sporting a brown hooded sweatshirt and a

Black Cleveland Browns Hat that he had taken from Kilo's closet.

In his head Steal had the robbery all planned out. Once the house was secured he would threaten to kill Kiki and her unborn baby if Freddie did not give up the stash. Then once he got the money, he would kill Black and take off with all of the cash. Steal had no intentions of harming any of Kilo's family, he owed him just that much. Steal snapped out of his callous, but justifiable scheme, and replied to Kiki, "I will shoot him. I don't give a fuck about that niggah. I needed a little help to pull this off, that's all. But if he hurts the old man or his wife, I will kill him. That's my word," Steal said while pulling back the gun from the side of Kiki's face and placing it on his lap.

The answer Steal gave confused Kiki, but it provided a sense of comfort to the situation. She watched intently as Black crept up onto the porch wearing Kilo's clothing, "Oh God Please!"

Kiki exploded into tears again. Steal remained silent- with a greedy grin on his face.

Before knocking on the door, Black rattled the doorknob to see if it was carelessly left unlocked. He then walked across the squeaky wooden porch to try and lift up the widow. It was locked too. Black peered through the window and was able to partially see into the living room.

Lisa quickly sat up in the bed after hearing an unusual noise coming from downstairs. She waited quietly, and then she heard the sounds again- as if someone was on the porch. Lisa turned to her left and started to shake her husband repeatedly. "Fred I think someone is downstairs. There's a noise coming from the porch or inside the house," she whispered.

It wasn't long before Freddie was hearing the same noises. Still half asleep, he eased out of bed with his wife and tip-toed to the closet. He quickly came out holding his shotgun tightly with both hands. His heart was racing. If Lisa had not been so frightened, she would have laughed when she noticed that while inside of the closet, Freddie had slipped on his green camouflaged army cap.

Lisa crawled out of bed and followed closely behind her husband. She was armed with a bottle of pepper spray. The couple cautiously made their way down the stairs. Once they reached the bottom of the steps, they could see the silhouette of a person standing outside of the door, knocking lightly. Freddie slowly walked across the living room and carefully lifted one blind and looked out of the window. From past devastation he made sure he would look out of a peep hole or a window before ever asking, "Who is it?" Years ago when he was shot six times, he had foolishly opened the door for the perpetrators who tried to take his life.

The first thing Freddie noticed about the strange man standing on his porch was the shiny pistol held behind the man's back. After registering the potential danger, Freddie signaled with a hand waive for Lisa to go back upstairs. Without hesitation she quickly complied.

Freddie noticed that the man was twisting the doorknob and then began ramming his shoulder into the door. He was trying to force his way inside. Freddie slowly moved towards the door. The hinges were loosening. His heart was racing. All Freddie could think about was protecting his wife. He slowly touched the end of his shotgun against the door- in front of the potential intruder.

The man rammed his shoulder into the door two more forceful times before the loud shot erupted (Boom!!). The shotgun blast roared throughout the quiet 19th Ward neighborhood. Dogs in every yard started howling at the sound that suddenly stole their solitude. Lights in other residences began to come on and doors cracked open slightly to see what in the hell was going on at the Miller's home.

"No. No!" Kiki screamed when she heard the blast. She grabbed the handle to the door and dove out as Steal ripped the hood from her coat, while trying to grab her. Without thinking Steal leaned over and fired two shots (Boom, Boom!!) in her direction. Kiki cried out in agony as one of the hot bullets passed through her flesh. The 300c's screeching tires left smoke in the middle of the street as

Steal nervously fled the scene.

Black died instantly as the slug pushed through his chest, sending him backwards off of the porch. He lay stretched out in the lawn, lifeless. Freddie heard the dead man's gun fall to the wooden porch, and then moments later he heard two shots fired down the street. Freddie cocked his shotgun, opened the door, and then slowly walked outside. He saw the dead man motionless in the grass and there was a speeding car making a right at the corner of the street.

Freddie bypassed the man in the yard and ran to the end of the sidewalk. He could see someone lying at the curb. The female voice was yelling for help. Freddie then sprinted to the rescue. "Lord Jesus! Keisha what happened to you?" he cried.

"I'm sorry Uncle Freddie. I'm so sorry," Kiki tearfully pleaded.

Freddie held her body in his arms. Kiki's entire white, fur coat was now covered in blood. Her eyes were nearly closed, as she continued to say, "I'm sorry."

Freddie yelled to a woman who had come outside with a phone in her hand, "Call the ambulance. My niece has been shot!"

CHAPTER TWENTY ONE
THE WEAK SHALL PARISH

"In life there will arise situations that were meant to break you. Its object is to cause you to make unwise decisions that will result in your downfall. In every walk of life there will be tribulation. In the end, a man is not defined by where he stood in the midst of his best moments, but more so by where he stood during the toughest times of his life..."

As quick as it had gotten bad for Kilo- it became much worse. He hadn't been to church in months, which had become a Sunday usual for him and Kiki. After all of his wicked deeds, selling drugs, killing Kay Cee, and sleeping with different women Kilo was afraid to get on his knees and talk to God. He was scared of what he might hear. He had continued breaking commandments while indulging in the ills of his street life after being chastened by the Lord. Kilo smoked more and more weed every day. The morals and principles he adapted while in jail had been quickly abandoned by the harsh realities of society. Jail helped Kilo to strive for positivity, but the elements of this cruel world made it impossible for one to successfully plan their future. *'How could you plan on staying positive when your right hand man was snitching? How could you really avoid having to kill him? How could you prepare for niggahs shooting your girl?'* Kilo thought.

Kilo felt as if the weight of the world was once again upon his shoulders. It was similar to his feelings while sitting in the Monroe County Jail facing murder charges. He had not seen or heard from Kiki since the shooting. From what he knew, she was at her mother's house recovering from a gunshot wound to her left arm. It marked his worse fear coming to life- Kiki being hurt because of his lifestyle. Now her mother, Diane, was determined to keep the two separated forever. It seemed as though there was nothing he could do to make this situation right again. After all what mother would really want their child's life being jeopardized by a major drug dealer.

The night of the shooting Renee called Kilo's cell phone, and hysterically cried, "Kilo where are you? Keisha's been shot! She's at the Strong Memorial Hospital in the emergency room now..." Kilo could not believe this had happened. At the time he wanted to ask so many questions but Renee quickly hung up the phone. Kilo jumped up from the bed, leaving a naked Moet alone in the hotel.

When Kilo finally arrived at the hospital he was the last person the family wanted to see, especially as far as Diane was concerned. Kilo could not believe that a Christian lady was capable of speaking that many curse words. Diane called him everything but the child of God. Kilo was in no mood to argue as he rushed towards the operating room. Diane jumped in his path, and shouted, "Stay the fuck away from my daughter! This whole thing is your fault Tymer!" She then grabbed onto Kilo's arm after he brushed past her. Kilo forcefully swung away from her grip, sending Diane falling down to the white marble floor. Smooth C rushed Kilo from the side with the rage of a bull. A fight began and before you knew it wild punches were exchanged between the two. The security immediately stopped the fight and escorted Kilo out of the hospital. He didn't even have the chance to see his childhood love.

This situation qualified as the worse time of Kilo's young life. He had been riding around the streets of Rochester all day in his brand new fire red Ferrari- smoking blunt after blunt. Kilo also spent $80,000 dollars on exclusive platinum jewelry that was filled with exotic diamonds. Splurging on diamonds and a new sports car was his way of telling the stick-up kids who shot Kiki "kiss my ass". Kilo wanted the streets to know that they will never stop the progress of a true hustler. On his lap rested a chrome .357 magnum and on the passenger's seat was a .38 special handgun with a brown wooden handle. Kilo was begging for the next attempt to rob him.

Kilo knew that niggahs couldn't hold onto water in the dessert and whoever shot Kiki would soon come to light. There was no need to threaten anyone for answers. Kilo would just wait and once someone gave him the name of the person responsible- their whole family would be at risk of early deaths. They could have shot him ten times, but to harm Kiki meant a murder spree.

Kilo wanted the stick-up kids to see him still shining- still winning, but now even harder. He didn't want to reveal to the hood how he really felt. Word was out about Kiki getting shot and everyone was wondering how Kilo would react. Kilo knew this. The Heights expected for Kilo to jump out with guns drawn on the block demanding answers or some typical crazy shit like it, but not this time. Kilo decided to flash money in the faces of the greedy. Failing was one thing but to see a niggah laughing when you expected them to cry made failure even harder to cope with. And Kilo hoped that this coupled with pride would cause the person who shot Kiki to reveal their hand.

The botched robbery that left Kiki shot had changed Kilo's game plan from 'get money and enjoy life' to 'find out who did it and get even'.

———————

"Fuck!" Kilo cursed into his rearview mirror. He quickly turned on the air conditioner in an attempt to clear out the thick weed smoke that filled the car's atmosphere. The red and blue lights spiraling behind his car reminded him of the day the police busted the drug house in Marketview Heights and brought him out in handcuffs.

Kilo slowly grabbed the .38 special and .357 together, and then slid them onto the back floor of the red coupe. He was not nervous at all. He felt as if his reign in the streets of Rochester, New York had now come to its end. Prison was inevitable based on the decisions he made after coming home from jail.

Kilo let his head fall back against the headrest as he placed both of his hands onto the wooden steering wheel. Besides the two illegal handguns in the car, there was also a quarter of a kilogram of cocaine inside the glove compartment. Kilo was on his way to sell the drugs to a well-known hustler on the Westside, but was stopped short by police as soon as he exited the highway on Ames Boulevard. He had been caught recklessly 'riding dirty' in a hundred thousand dollar sports car.

The tall white officer cautiously approached the fancy sports car with one hand shining his flashlight into the small vehicle and the other hand holding onto the handle of his gun. Kilo cracked the window just enough to be able to hear what the timid cop had to say. "Can I see your license and registration please, sir?" The officer asked nicely.

Officer Dearcoff only pulled over the red Ferrari because of the young black face that was driving. He himself loved sports cars and was curious to see who was behind the wheel of a car that his salary couldn't afford. The officer was blinded by Kilo's diamond necklace, bracelet, watch, and rings. He could smell the faint odor of marijuana coming from the car, and then he became certain that the young man was a major drug dealer.

"Of course you could see my license, but do you have a reason for stopping me?" Kilo asked. "And please don't say because I'm black."

"No sir. Your race has nothing to do with this traffic stop. A few blocks back you cruised through a red light without stopping. Now could I have your license, please?" Dearcoff said growing impatient.

Kilo reluctantly pulled his wallet from his back pocket and slid his license through the space he left in the window. He knew at this point the police really had no reason to search his car. It was one of the benefits to having a valid driver's license. Officer Dearcoff gave Kilo a suspicious look before he turned and walked back towards his police cruiser to run Kilo's government name for any possible warrants.

Kilo was upset because it took the officer so long to return. He picked up his cell phone and was in the process of calling his Uncle Freddie when he heard a loud crashing sound. "What the fuck!" Kilo shouted. The officer had smashed out the left tail light of Kilo's car with his club. At that very moment police cars swarmed around the area from all directions. They were surrounding Kilo like furious bees.

"Slowly, get the fuck out of the vehicle!" Dearcoff demanded by aiming his gun at Kilo.

Kilo couldn't even count the amount of police cars that arrived in the matter of seconds. He thought about grabbing his two guns and holding court in the streets. But that was quickly overshadowed by the image of him lying in a casket, surrounded by his family. 'Am I really ready to die?'

The cops crept closer with their guns drawn, and yelling, "Put your fucking hands up!" Kilo looked at the serious facial expressions from the boys in blue and realized that he was not ready to die- especially not at the hands of the Rochester Police Department.

Kilo slowly put his hands up and then opened his car door. The police forcefully snatched him out of the car and slammed him to the hard pavement of the street. Once Kilo was handcuffed, two officers led him to an awaiting police cruiser. Kilo dropped his head when the door was slammed on him in the back seat. He knew that he was headed back to jail. A place he vowed to never return.

Soon, Kilo found himself sitting in a cold interrogation room on the fourth floor of the Public Safety building. It seemed to have been an eternity, but was actually only six hours of being handcuffed to a wooden table by one arm. Kilo had just fallen asleep as he waited.

"Hey, wake the fuck up boy!" FBI agent Benny Thompson

screamed. Kilo awoke to the sight of a white and a black man seated at the table before him. They were both smiling.

"Look like you got yourself in a lot of trouble young man. But there is no need to worry. We are here to help. I'm federal agent Mike Ledgeworth and this is my longtime partner Benny Thompson. We just want to ask you a few questions and maybe you could help us get to the bottom of this mess."

"If you think I am about to snitch, you got the wrong niggah. Hell would freeze first before a niggah like me flip. I have never told on anyone in my whole fucking life," Kilo said proudly.

Once Kilo finished saying his peace, Mike Ledgeworth began fumbling through a brown folder that had a U.S. Government stamp on the front. Kilo observed that inside the folder was paperwork and photos. The FBI agent started tossing pictures onto the table in front of him. The first familiar face was Kay Cee. Then he recognized those of the Dominicans, himself, Reggie, and a few other people he saw around the city at one time or another. The small, stuffy interrogation room remained silent as Kilo took his time to examine each photo.

When he was satisfied, he broke the silence by saying, "And? What the fuck is this supposed to mean?"

Benny Thompson leaned forward over the table with his face twisted up into his usual frown and said, "Nigger, it means life in jail for conspiracy. And after your stupid black ass die you will still owe us time for those guns and cocaine we found in your car!"

Kilo knew that he was in a no win situation but needed to keep his composure. He had to think of something to say quickly, "All you got is pictures. Yea, Kay Cee was a friend of mines. I knew him for years. He did whatever he did before his death, but I never sold drugs in my life. The guns in the car were mines... I needed them as I feared for my life in the streets, but I have no idea what cocaine you're talking about."

That was his best attempt at denouncing his criminal activity. Kilo wanted to see just how much the FBI knew, and agent Mike

Ledgeworth was more than happy to let him know.

"You see Mr. Miller or do you prefer to be called Kilo, short for kilogram? But anyways, we know everything about you. Keisha Jackson, she's your girlfriend of ten years, isn't she? We're sorry to hear about her being shot last week. We were glad to see that the baby survived the shooting and the rest of the pregnancy will be fine. The doctors did a great job," Mike Ledgeworth said.

"Well you do know something that I don't because Keisha isn't pregnant at all... What does all of this bullshit have to do with why I'm here anyways?"

Benny Thompson rocked back and forth in his chair as he was killing Kilo with his eyes. He was trying his best to intimidate him. He got up and walked around the table, and then leaned over Kilo's left shoulder, and said sternly, "We ask the questions, boy!"

Agent Ledgeworth continued, "We must admit that you're a real gangster. We haven't seen your character around in Rochester for a long while. You have managed to get away with a lot in Marketview Heights, haven't you?" Kilo did not answer. "I'm still confused though Mr. Miller. Why would you kill Kenny Conway after he bumped off Danasha Graham in order for you to be acquitted of murder two? I mean- is that how you repay friends?"

Kilo sat back in his chair with his free arm folded behind his head. Agent Thompson was still hovering over him. Kilo didn't want to say anything that would tie him to other crimes besides the guns and cocaine in his car. So he decided to listen.

"And to be honest, that's where you basically screwed up. Kenny Conway was a good friend of ours. I'm sure you heard about it. Maybe that's why you did away with him. Before Kenny died, he did have a lot of things to say about you. Would you care to hear a few words from your late friend?" Mike Ledgeworth asked.

Kilo shook his head "no" fearing what he might hear, but Benny Thompson pulled a small tape out of his inside coat pocket and pushed it into a cassette player that was on the table. Kilo hadn't heard Kay Cee's voice in a while but he knew immediately that it was him. Hearing Kay Cee speak brought back many memories. It was like talking to him on speaker phone, but only now the words he spoke was unlike him.

"Yea Omar his real name but I never knew his last name." Benny Thompson pressed fast forward. *"..exactly how many kilograms of cocaine did you say Tymer Miller could sell in a month?... about ten. His business is at an all-time high. Kilo's not the only one making a lot of money in these streets. You got Reggie..."* Thompson slammed his finger down on the stop button.

Kilo was furious. Kay Cee deserved to die. He was really telling on everyone. Years, months, and days in federal prison passed through Kilo's traveling mind. He knew how the Feds operated and with just this bullshit evidence he could get fried at trial. He also knew that this was not their entire case. If he went to trail, hustlers he sold crack to years ago would be in court to testify on him. That's just how it worked. The Feds would show a defendant just enough to make a niggah think they can beat the case, and then hand you your balls in court. *'Who will take care of Kiki and Freddie if I don't cooperate?'* Kilo thought.

At this very moment Kilo could almost understand what Kay Cee was going through when he was being tricked by these same federal agents. He vividly remembered his last conversation with Kay Cee before he pulled the trigger and ended his life. "It's two FBI agents. One name is Benny Thompson and the other is Mike Ledgeworth. They broke me down Kilo. They threatened me with five hundred months... In my mind I had no choice," Kay Cee cried. Pressure made diamonds but in Kay Cee's case it burst his pipes. Right then Kilo knew what he had to do. It would only be for the people he loved. It was for the fact that he could now relate to Kay Cee's struggle. Kilo had to make the best decision in regards to his freedom.

"So how could you help me to get out of this shit? I'm too young. I don't have time to spend locked away in prison... What do you want from me?" Kilo asked desperately, as he sat up and folded his arms on the table.

The glow of defeat was written all over Kilo's brown face. It was deep in his expressions that he had given up and was ready to trade sides. Both agents' faces lit up with excitement. Even Benny Thompson was unusually showing his yellow, coffee stained teeth under a rare smile. From behind Kilo's back, Benny Thompson gave his partner the thumbs up. They had done it again in their collective thirty years on the job. They successfully flipped another weak minded drug dealer into cooperation.

In harmony both agents sung the same words, "Give us Omar and we guarantee you will walk!"

CHAPTER TWENTY TWO
THE STRONG WILL
SURVIVE

"The bottom is a form of weakness, but to occupy a spot at the top of your field you must possess an incredible amount of strength. To be respected at your craft your power to maintain a worry free mind in tough situations must be visible to those who are trying to bring you down. Their advantage is your weakness, but their weakness is not realizing the capabilities of your strengths. A thinking man will understand and he will always remain at the top..."

Today was Kiki's first day back to work. She had given all of the girls who worked for her the day off. Dominique, Alexis, and Jasmine were more than pleased when Kiki called to say they could stay home this morning. The woman had worked six days a week just to keep the hair salon afloat while their extremely lenient boss recovered. Kiki's arm still bothered her but she wanted to get back to work today knowing that she owed it to her clientele.

Everyone who came into the salon asked about Kilo. No one had seen him in days. Kiki herself had not heard from him since the shooting. Tasha called a week and a half ago to say she saw Kilo ride past her house driving a red sports car. She described the car as being very expensive. And that was the last time anyone had reported seeing Kilo.

Kiki didn't want to think that anything bad happened to Kilo. If he had been in jail, surely he would have contacted her by now. Or the unthinkable- he might be dead. Kiki stopped braiding Adrian's hair for a second. She stepped back and softly held the sides of her growing stomach. "Please God don't let anything have happened to Kilo. What was done to me wasn't his fault. Please God."

"Kiki you okay?" Adrian asked in a concerned voice. He was one of her regular customers. All he ever wanted was small braids to the back of his head.

"Yes honey. I am okay. My baby was just kicking," Kiki replied while rubbing her stomach.

"I didn't know you were pregnant Kiki."

"Yes sir. Four months now," she said as she twisted his final braid.

Adrian stood up, observed his braids in the mirror, and then pulled out a wad of cash from his pocket. He peeled off a crisp hundred dollar bill and handed it to Kiki. "This is an early gift for the baby. Tell Kilo and your brother Smooth C I said, what up."

"I will," Kiki said as she stuffed the Benjamin inside of her bra.

Adrian was Kiki's last customer of the day. Kiki picked up a broom and began sweeping. While she was busy cleaning behind the chair, she heard a roar of excitement coming from the barber shop next door. Kiki stopped sweeping for a moment and walked to the big doorway that separated the barber shop from the beauty salon. Her heart skipped a beat when she saw Kilo slapping fives and greeting the hustlers that were getting haircuts. He spoke to a couple people, and then continued to the back towards the salon.

Kiki was rushing to put on her fur coat when Kilo walked in. She was fronting like she didn't see him coming.

"What's up Kiki," Kilo said softly.

Kiki slowly turned around to face him. She looked Kilo up and down. He looked kind of rough to be a man who was so concerned with his appearance. He had stubble growing on his face and his

Allen Iverson braids were raggedy. Kiki had never seen him looking like this before. She could tell that he had just finished smoking a blunt because his eyes were blood shot red- and he smelled like a pound of weed. Kilo was wearing a brand new fatigue sweat suit and two diamond necklaces she didn't know he had.

"Nothing much, I was just about to leave. What brings you here?" Kiki asked.

"This is my shop, right?" Kilo asked. "Kiki I came to the hospital to see you, but your family flipped. So I left. I am so happy you are okay. I miss you so much."

"So you don't call or nothing? But you care so much, huh?"

"Look Kiki I swear I have been going through so much lately. You just don't know. I heard you were fine so I just wanted to give you space- hoping you would call me," Kilo said.

"Niggah please, I had just been shot and my man was nowhere to be found. Fuck what my mom was saying, I needed you," Kiki pleaded as a tear escaped from her soul.

Kilo looked down and stared at her stomach. He noticed that her white shirt was fitting extra tight. Kilo observed that her cheeks were fatter and her breast had gotten larger. "Kiki, are you pregnant?" She put her head down. She was embarrassed. Kiki began to cradle her stomach- giving Kilo his answer.

"You should've told me... I am so happy," Kilo said with a bright smile.

"I was trying to figure out a way to tell you before all of this shit happened. I'm four months baby."

Kilo grabbed Kiki into his embrace. She felt so good to be able to hold again. Her womanly scent brought back memories of love, sex, and happiness. Things never seemed so bad when he was wrapped up in her arms.

"Damn! Kilo, be careful with my arm boy," Kiki said as she was being squeezed too close by her healing gunshot wound.

"Oh, I'm sorry," Kilo said. "I promise that I am going to find out who was the other dude involved. I know they both aren't from

Buffalo. The one who got away has to be from the town. Word to my dead sister Kim I'm going to body that niggah!"

"Kilo those niggahs had me scared to death. They threatened to rape and kill me if I didn't tell them where the money was… It's a true blessing that me and the baby still alive. When was the last time you spoke to Freddie?"

"I talked to him earlier today. They moved into a new house out in Chili. He told me to tell you hello and get well soon," Kilo said. "Are you mad at me still?"

Kiki thought for a second, and said, "Not anymore. I cried for a week straight worrying about what you would do to retaliate. My mom insisted for me to stay away from you, but I love you too much to ever leave you. It sounds stupid, but I am proud I took a bullet for my niggah. I would rather have been shot and lived- then you had been shot and killed. That's how I look at it."

"You are the best. And I came to deliver some good news," Kilo said with a smile.

"Really, what is it?" Kiki asked as she wrapped her arms around his waist.

"You remember when we were in Florida with Omar and you said you wanted to move?" Kilo asked.

"Yes Tymer, I remember."

"We're leaving tomorrow. We have to get far away from Rochester."

To Kiki this news was better than Kilo asking for her hand in marriage. She longed to escape the harsh reality of living in the City of Rochester. And now that she was about to bring a child into the world, Kilo could not have picked a better time.

"I love you," Kiki said as she passionately kissed his lips. Their tongues wrestled as Kilo felt over her soft body.

Kilo instructed Kiki to pack the things she needed and to be ready to leave by 8:00 pm tomorrow. He informed her to give Renee their house keys and to leave her the Benz too. Also, he wanted Dominique to run the salon.

Genesee Valley Park was a local Westside recreation center for the ghetto youths who lived in its vicinity. Outside of the center was a huge beautiful park that was equipped with an Olympic size swimming pool, basketball courts, and a large picnic area. Parents from all over the city brought their kids here to play during the warm summer months. Due to the late hour and cold weather the recreation center was deserted.

The only individuals who strolled around the park tonight were undercover law enforcement officers- representing almost every local branch. The tall white man who was walking a big German Sheppard was a member of the FBI. Agents Mike Ledgeworth and long-time partner Benny Thompson gathered into a small white minivan at the corner of Brooks Avenue along with four other agents. They were anticipating the perfect moment to send the "go" command.

Unmarked police cars circled the surrounding area of the park. The Rochester Police Department had a special drug enforcement team on standby to help assist in the apprehension of Rochester's most notorious drug dealer. They've wanted to see this man in handcuffs for years, but he had proven to be elusive by using his street smarts to avoid doing anything to warrant a federal indictment. Although he was not a violent criminal- he sure as hell was a prosperous one. He made millions of dollars by selling crack cocaine during the 1990's. He single handedly paved the way for hundreds of hustlers to profit from Rochester's drug market. But today would mark the end of his reign as a drug kingpin. The FBI strongly felt they flipped the right hustler, someone extremely close to him and has a lot to lose. Kilo had his freedom, reputation, and family on the line and the Feds believed it was all they needed to bring down the king himself, Omar Langley.

Earlier this morning, Kilo was forced to use his FBI monitored

cell phone to call Omar. He spoke in the same code words he in-
formed the agents he would, "Omar I need you to take my *two*
daughters to the center today... I will meet you at the Genesee
Valley Park at eight o'clock to pick them up," Kilo said. Translation:
*Omar bring me two kilograms of cocaine to the Genesee Valley
Park at 8:00 p.m.* Omar agreed.

The agreement itself was enough to charge Omar with conspiracy to sell two kilograms of cocaine, along with Kilo's testimony.
Kilo refused to wear a wire during the transaction due to the danger
involved, but he promised to testify against Omar for a reduced
sentence on his own federal gun and drug charges.

Benny Thompson was the first to spot the black Yukon Denali
pulling into the huge parking lot. Kilo described it as the vehicle
Omar would be driving. "He has a lot of cars but he mainly drives
the black Yukon during the winter," Kilo told. Because it was so
dark outside the agent had to adjust the lens on his camera to get
a closer shot. Mike Ledgeworth began taking pictures of the black
SUV. In the same instance, the dark blue Nissan Maxima Kilo said
he would be driving pulled up alongside of Omar's truck. It was 7:58
p.m.

Benny Thompson held his walkie-talkie close to his mouth, and
said, "Everyone get into position. Await my signal!"

The suspect looked around carefully as he exited the Maxima.
He was holding a big brown paper bag in his left hand that was filled
with $56,000 dollars' worth of marked money. After Kilo described
both vehicles, he said that he would be wearing a black hooded
sweatshirt underneath a black leather jacket. And that's exactly
what he had on as Mike Ledgeworth began secretly taking pictures
of the ghetto celebrity as if he wore paparazzi.

"We should have never let Miller wear that damn hood. I can't
get any clear shots of him at all," Ledgeworth complained.

"Don't worry partner we have all we need already. We got
the taped phone call to Langley and now the two kilos of coke.
This motherfuckah has no light at the end of his tunnel," Benny

Thompson said, and then broke out into a hysterical laugh. Soon the other agents in the van were laughing as well.

Their suspect jumped into the passenger's seat of the Denali, kicking snow from his Timberland field boots before slamming the door behind him. Agent Benny Thompson yelled into his walkie-talkie, "Go now! Go now!"

The lady sitting at the bus stop dropped her newspaper, jumped up, and then pulled a big gun from her wool coat. The man walking his dog dropped the leash and pulled a pistol from his waist. Sirens suddenly illuminated the area. The white caravan raced into the parking lot carrying Thompson and Ledgeworth. The van abruptly slid to a screeching halt behind Omar's truck. Rochester's Narcotics Unit jumped out of a beige van seconds before it came to a complete stop. The FBI agents along with all of the other law enforcement agencies on the scene approached the black SUV on foot with their weapons drawn and ready to fire.

"Freeze!" ordered the officers as they neared. "Don't fucking move!"

Seeing that both suspects had their hands in the air, Benny Thompson snatched open the passenger door. His evil eyes met the blank stare of an unfamiliar face. "Who in the fuck are you?" Thompson angrily shouted while lowering his pistol.

"I'm your worse fucking nightmare. This is for Kay Cee!" the young black male said as he quickly reached between his legs and drew a .45 caliber handgun. The driver who was not Omar came from his inside coat pocket with a small Mack 11 (Boom xxx!). He began spraying rounds of bullets through the truck's windows at every police officer in his sight. The passenger managed to squeeze one bullet (boom!) into the neck of Benny Thompson, before retaliatory bullets riddled through the windows and mettle of the Yukon.

Police officers stood and fired cartridge after cartridge into the bodies of the two suspects. Genesee Valley Park sounded as if it was home to an early New Year's Eve fireworks event.

The driver of the truck was able to kill three officers before a farewell bullet blasted him in his face. The passenger, Rah Rah, laid slumped over as his poor body continued to be filled with lead. He had just come home from serving ten months at the Westfall Detention Center for adolescents.

The FBI and RPD would be ridiculed for months to come for their carelessness in killing a fifteen year old minor in a so-called, 'Major drug bust'.

"Cease fire!" Mike Ledgeworth screamed.

The loud crackling sounds of bullets slowly simmered as each officer took their final shot into the vehicle.

"Fuck. Fuck!" Ledgeworth yelled as he slammed his fist into the nearest police cruiser. He would never forget the bloodshed before him. Mike Ledgeworth scanned the scene. He cried as he let his eyes rest on the sight of his partner Benny Thompson lying dead in a pool of his own blood. He thought of Kilo, Tymer Miller, who he knew to be the orchestrator of this deadly night. He vowed to spend the rest of his career bringing Kilo back to justice…

CHAPTER TWENTY THREE
WE OUT THE HOOD NOW

"**Nothing in life last forever! Sometimes the events that take place in our lives are just signs of what's to come. This game was never meant to be a career and no black man needed to die in order to get money. There has always been enough for everyone. But the bad has meaning. Just maybe the top is ready to be occupied by another- and just maybe you're risking your life as you do all in your power to stay relevant in the streets. A smart boxer fights to win, but a great one understands when to throw in the towel. Take it from me. I have been through it all... The life of a true hustler...!" - $$Mike**

With Kilo missing in action Smooth C inherited the throne. At only eighteen he was now responsible for supplying all of Marketview Heights with crack cocaine. He enjoyed being the man. And even though he wasn't speaking to Kilo, he still missed having him around in the hood. It just wasn't the same. It's been two weeks since Smooth C last saw his sister Kiki. He missed her the most. She was the next best thing to a caring mother. Kiki gave him her new phone number and made Smooth C promise to keep in touch. "Stay out of trouble little bra'," she told him before leaving their mother's house on the night she departed.

A lot of shit has happened since Kilo fled from the city. It proved that without a strong leader the hood would eventually lose its unity and loyalty. Among the bullshit, the twins Ronald and Donald was killed in a drive by shooting in front of the Mini Mart. They say it was the stick up kids from over the bridge who was responsible, but like always no one was arrested. On top of that, the fiend lady Debbie overdosed in the University building last week. Everyone who was smoking crack with her ran out of the apartment and left her for dead. She was one of Anne's close friends. Not too long ago, one of Smooth C's workers ran off with twenty eight balls, and then the next day niggahs shot up his new Benz at the club.

The Heights was still mourning the death of Lil' Rah Rah. Hustlers from the hood acted a fool at his wake. They started pouring beer and alcohol over his body like it was really the way to lay a fifteen year old boy to rest. Sadly, his only family in attendance was the hood. Life is rough. Since Rah Rah's death every police car that came through the hood was either shot at or bombarded with rocks and bottles. In a matter of weeks the hood was in turmoil.

Smooth C was the only hustler who was selling major weight in Marketview Heights. He could feel the hate and tension in the hearts of so many hustlers. Respect was no longer a factor as niggahs became hungrier by the day and being that Kilo and Kay Cee was out of the picture, the goons was ready to feed.

Being that it was a drought in Rochester, Smooth C was forced to raise his prices much higher than what Kilo was selling coke for. In many ways being a major niggah was harder than expected. Kilo once admonished from jail, "Smooth C one day you may be forced to take over the hood. All you have to do is stay focused and hustle hard. The hood will soon grow to love you!"

Smooth C was beginning to think of getting out of the game himself after seeing so many hustlers fall. He didn't want to make the game a career and end up dead like Kay Cee or on the run like Kilo. The only thing holding him back from walking away was the fact that his money wasn't long enough to quit. He was only sitting on $60,000 dollars in cash and a kilogram of crack he had in the streets for sale. During Smooth C's short run as a hustler all he ever wanted to do with the money he made was buy cars and expensive jewelry- instead of putting the illegal cash away somewhere safe for a rainy day. Now when he was having a feeling in his gut that it was time to leave the game alone, it was the lack of sufficient funds standing in his way.

There was only one good thing happening in Smooth C's world and that was his relationship with Foxy. She was really the one who had been encouraging him to leave the streets while he was still young. To her, sixty thousand dollars was more than enough to give up selling drugs, but to a hustler that much money wasn't shit. Foxy wanted to move to New York City and go back to school, work, and save money until they found another city to settle down. Her suggestions sounded wonderful, but Smooth C knew that nothing actually happens the way they were planned.

Foxy had a troubled background that made it easy for her to be understanding to the struggle. She told Smooth C of all the drama she had been through growing up in her projects. After being raped by her mother's boyfriend at the age of ten she ran away from home and winded up staying in drug houses having sex with hustlers much older than she- just for weed and food. Even though she admitted to doing some real degrading shit, Smooth C still loved her. He understood how easy it was for a female to get turned out in Rochester. He had been with many women in the past two years and none of them was any better than Foxy. What made her different was the fact that she wanted more out of life and actually had dreams.

Smooth C rolled over in his bed and looked at the clock. It was two o'clock in the morning. As he lay awake next to Foxy he was hoping that the blunt he was smoking would help him sleep. However, the good weed only caused his mind to travel deeper into the thoughts that were keeping him up. Smooth C's problems in the streets were one thing but it couldn't compare to what Foxy had told him earlier in the day. He kept thinking about what she said and how it made him have to beat her ass today. He hit her with everything from vicious slaps to painful kicks in her small ribs.

Smooth C never had to hit a woman before until Foxy decided to tell him about Steal and what she over heard him say one day. Smooth C went crazy. He even went as far as putting his Desert Eagle handgun to her head, threatening to kill her if she wasn't telling the truth. The only thing that saved her young life today was the stream of tears that rolled down her chocolate face. Smooth C lowered his gun, and said, "What am I doing? Why would you lie about something like this?"

"I wouldn't... Cedric baby I wouldn't lie," Foxy said between tears.

"I know Foxy. I'm sorry, but you should have been told me this shit when we first met. Now, Kilo will think that I knew this whole time and didn't tell him."

"Well, then don't."

"I have too," Smooth C replied while shaking his head.

Foxy was now sleeping in bed next to him with her thumb in her mouth and a yellow scarf wrapped around her head. Tonight after the fight she made Smooth C shed some tears too. After showering she climbed in bed with him and began kissing his body from the lips- slowly down his stomach. She said, "Cedric, the difference be- tween me sucking Steal's dick and yours is that I love you. He damn near forced me to do that for him. Now I am all yours. He'll get what he deserves very soon."

She touched Smooth C with her honesty and he cried while she continued down his body until her mouth covered his erection.

What Foxy failed to realize is that Smooth C did not attack her for giving Steal some head. That was before him and could have easily been forgiven. What evoked his anger was when she said, "I heard Steal say that he killed Kilo's sister before he went to jail and he told the guy he was with that when they rob Kilo, he would be next... Baby Steal was drunk and saying all kinds of crazy shit that night."

Smooth C knew that what Foxy told him had the potential to cause a lot of bloodshed. Being that Steal was the one who shot his own sister- he wanted to kill him, but this was much more personal for Kilo.

Smooth C pulled in a lung full of weed smoke and said out loud in the darkness of his room, "Steal, you will get touched."

———=((()))=———

From the very start Kilo never intended to snitch on anyone, especially not Omar. He was responsible for Kilo being successful at selling so much crack cocaine in Marketview Heights. Kilo knew that nothing good comes to a person who bit the hand that fed them. Kilo made sure to tell the Feds only enough to stay inside of their comfort zone until he could make a power move. He needed time on the streets to formulate a plan and the only way that could happen was if he gave the impression he would cooperate.

Once the FBI let Kilo out on an ankle bracelet, it didn't take long for him to decide on the best get away. He also wanted to get revenge on the agents who flipped his longtime friend, Kay Cee. Kilo blamed them for his death.

A few weeks ago when Lil Rah Rah was released from the Juvenile Detention Center on the drug and gun charges he took for Kilo, he came back to the hood broke and looking for work. Instead of giving him more crack to sell, Kilo gave him $2,500 dollars in cash as a welcome home gift. Kilo said, "Take this money and stay low out here. You just came home and don't need to be hustling yet. But I will get with you if I really need you, son."

Lil Rah Rah replied, "No doubt Kilo. You know I will do anything for you my niggah."

So when Kilo began planning his escape from Rochester, naturally Lil Rah Rah came to mind. Klev was another thorough young niggah from the hood. Kilo used to fuck his older sister, Stacy, a few years ago. Klev was perfect for the job because he looked just like Omar. He was just twenty years younger. Kilo promised the two hungry teens five thousand dollars apiece for them to drive to Genesee Valley park in Omar's Denali and a rented Maxima. Kilo warned that the police would run up on them, but by the time they figure out what was going on he'd be doing 100mph on 390 south.

Kilo then called Omar from a nearby pay phone, "O-."

"What's up my niggah?" Omar said as he recognized his pro-tégé's voice.

"Listen, this is going to be real brief. You got to go man. It's serious. The Feds are trying to get me to flip on you. Don't worry I'm calling from a pay phone and I will die before I turn bitch… you know that!" Kilo said nervously. "I need for you to leave your Denali in the old G & G's Steakhouse parking lot with the keys underneath the driver's seat. All of this shit is behind Kay Cee snitching ass. You was right, niggahs can be hoes too. I'm sorry I didn't listen to you."

"Don't worry Kilo. No apologies needed. I respect the game to the fullest. They have been trying to get me for years. I love that you have decided to keep it gangstah' with me. The truck will be there in a couple hours. You be safe and always remember that vindictiveness and greed leads to death and incarceration," Omar admonished before he disconnected.

That conversation was a month ago and now Kilo was trying to adapt to his new life. Kilo and Kiki was now known as the Parkers. They were a married couple from Grand Rapids, Michigan. At first Kiki didn't like her new name, Imoni, until Kilo explained that it meant to believe with all your heart in the people, parents, teachers, and the righteousness and victory of your struggle. Kiki then thought it to be a deep name and stopped complaining. She started to laugh when she asked Kilo to explain the meaning of his new name, Jermaine.

The Parkers was living off of the $1M dollars Kilo had buried in his backyard. The money was brilliantly saved for rainy days. Kilo bought a two bedroom home in West Palm Beach, Florida. He planned on living in it until after the baby was born, and then they would use their fake passports and sail across the ocean to Cuba.

Kiki loved her home, her new life, and even more Kilo. She couldn't wait for the baby to be born so she could flee the country. Kilo had been spoiling her with jewelry, gifts, and shopping sprees ever since they left Rochester. She felt like a queen. However, she was a little home sick. Kiki really missed her mother, brother, and friends Tasha and Renee. Everybody thinks they moved to NYC. The only person who knew the truth was Smooth C. He calls once in a while to update her on the hood and their mother's health.

Kiki understood that leaving her loved ones and her family behind was a sacrifice she needed to make in order to keep her family together. She realized that Kilo was on the run. But no matter where or how long he ran, she vowed to be jogging right by his side. She would just hope and pray that one day she could return to Rochester, NY just to visit.

"Kilo, when we get to Cuba you should get back in school or something. You are not going over there to do anything illegal. We going there to get away and enjoy life with our child. The last thing I need is more drama," Kiki warned. She was sitting on the couch in their huge living room, while Kilo was on his knees in front of her kissing the roundness of her caramel coated stomach.

"Listen baby, I'm done with all that street shit. I left it behind in Rochester. I'm a millionaire. What else do I need?" Kiki shrugged her shoulders. "I have you and my unborn seed to love and care for. Money means a lot to me, but it can't buy true love and happiness," Kilo said as he kissed her stomach twice more.

"I guess I am just curious because we've been through so much in these past few months and I would hate for something to happen to you in Cuba- leaving me stuck in a foreign country alone with a fake passport!"

Kilo started laughing when he imagined her getting caught at the airport in Cuba with a bogus passport and being refused entrance back into the United States.

"Kiki you would be mad as hell. I could see you now trying to plead your case with the Cubans, 'I'm from Rochester, New York. I'm a U.S citizen!' Then they'll be like, 'No, no, no passport no good!'" Kilo joked. "But don't worry about that while you're pregnant. We going over there to chill and hopefully everything will be fine."

Kilo lifted the fabric of her long t-shirt over Kiki's breast. She wasn't wearing a bra so they hung nicely atop her stomach. He took the darkness of her right nipple into his mouth and softly sucked on it. Kiki put her hands behind his head and guided him down to where she desired him the most. She helped Kilo slide off her purple cotton panties, and then wrapped her arms behind both of her knees- holding up her own legs. Kilo dove into her love pool tongue first. He savored her sweet juices as he licked around the insides of her opening. Kiki closed her eyes and let out deep moans of pleasure. She bit the bottom of her lip to keep from screaming. Kilo flicked his tongue back and forth over her swelling clit. It didn't take long before her body began to tremble uncontrollably as she wrapped her strong legs around her lover's neck. He fought to raise her legs, but she forced him to remain emerged in her womanhood throughout her climax.

Kilo stood up and quickly removed his boxers. Standing in front of his beautiful woman, Kiki pulled him forward by his ass cheeks using both of her hands. He walked straight into her welcoming mouth. She began to twist her head, lick, and slob all around his dick until he couldn't take the pleasure anymore. "Daddy fuck me from behind. But not too hard because you might hurt the baby," She joked, then stood up and turned around before him. Kiki stretched her arms out to the back of the couch for support, arched her lower back, and then raised her ass up for Kilo. He rubbed his head around her wet vulva before he slowly plunged deep inside of her pussy. She screamed as she tried to run away from the extra inches that she didn't ask for- but he chased her, and flowed in and out until he filled her insides.

Kilo laid behind Kiki on the couch feeling drained. His shaft was pressed up against her soft ass, while he thought of things to make it rise again for a round two.

"Kilo," Kiki said while grabbing his arm and wrapping it around her body so that he could rub her stomach. "I was just wondering if you would ever consider going back to Rochester. You know… after a couple years when all of this drama dies down."

Kilo thought about it for a moment, but before he could answer Kiki's cell phone started ringing on the table. She leaned forward and answered, "Hello." She listened to the other person on the phone for a few seconds, and then Kiki passed the phone over to Kilo, and said, "It's my brother Cedric. He asked for you… Be nice."

THE END... R.O.C Hard the life of a true hustler!!
Look forward to 'R.O.C Hard 2 a hustler's revenge...' 2016

www.mpowellbooks.com
www.facebook.com/MAPBOOKS777
@mapbooks
Instagram: @biggmike777

Author $$Mike Fanmail
P.O Box 30571
Rochester, New York 14603

CPSIA information can be obtained at www.ICGtesting.com
Printed in the USA
BVOW03s0250280414

351811BV00001B/1/P